A NOT SO HAPPY CAMPER

HOLT JACOBS MYSTERY - BOOK 6

LILY STIRLING

~ To Melissa ~

Your excitement about this story inspired my words.

CONTENTS

CHAPTER 1

"Holt, are you sure?" my baby sister, Juniper, asked. "Brittany knows you love her. You don't need to prove anything."

I ran a hand through my wavy blond hair. Some version of Juniper's words had played through my head thousands of times in the past few weeks.

They say love will make you do crazy things...But was giving up indoor plumbing really necessary?

I *really* didn't want to hike up a mountain with a thirty-pound pack on my back, only to spend my nights sleeping on the ground in a four-person tent—which couldn't comfortably fit three people.

"Come on, Holt, this is your last chance to back out."

Juniper's voice sounded almost normal, yet something in her tone made me take a closer look. My sister has the inhuman ability to always look perfect—with or without makeup. It's part of the reason she makes her living on social media. But behind the perfect facade, Juniper was biting her lip, and her forehead was wrinkled.

Huh.

Juniper was easily amused by my pain and was unafraid of pushing me into scrapes. She's orchestrated me sleeping on a plastic mattress protector and graffitied my Christmas stocking. Yet this wasn't an act. She wasn't trying to start a fight between me and my girlfriend. No,

Juniper was genuinely concerned I wouldn't survive a few days in the wild.

"Hey, I'll be fine." I put all of my big-brother overconfidence into the words—the sunglasses hid my dread.

Juniper wrinkled her nose. "Please, Holt. I remember how whiny you were when we stayed at a cabin that didn't have running water." She shuddered dramatically at the memory. "It was like the world was ending because you couldn't shower. This time, not only are there no showers, but instead of an outhouse, you'll have to shovel anytime you need to...*use* the restroom."

My jaw twitched. Needing a shovel for longer bathroom visits was high on the list of negatives—that and being eaten by bears.

My girlfriend's twin brother, Paul Asato, walked up, already wearing his backpack. He was taller than Britt but shared her dark hair and brown eyes...and was annoyingly handsome, with the broad shoulders of a commercial fisherman. "Is Juniper talking you out of backpacking?" Paul asked casually, yet I got the impression he couldn't believe I'd agreed to this.

"No way," I said, my eyes moving past him to where his girlfriend, Sienna, and Britt were walking to the park bathroom. "I'm all in."

Before Paul could answer, my phone lit up.

I groaned.

Mom was calling.

Oh no.

Due to my parents experiencing a midlife crisis and moving to Australia, Mom calling me in the early morning for Pacific time meant it was the middle of the night for her.

"Hello?" I asked.

"Good, I caught you," Mom said as a greeting.

What did she want? To check whether I was wearing sunscreen?

"Did you need something?" I asked. My voice was gruff.

"Not exactly. I just wanted you to know, Dad and I are proud of you for trying new things."

"Umm..."

What was that supposed to mean? I'd graduated with honors and have a successful engineering career. Was backpacking really the time Mom chose to be proud of me?

"Thanks, I guess."

In the distance Dad said, "I'm sure they're about to start. Tell Holt we love him and hang up."

Mom asked Dad, "Shouldn't we check if he's sure about the trip?"

Since Mom likely thought she'd covered the speaker, I cleared my throat.

"Oh, Holt heard—" Mom began to say when Dad came on the line. "We love you. Be safe. Have fun."

Sometimes my dad's ability to smooth over awkward family moments was truly astounding.

"Yeah," I said. "Love you, too. Bye."

Juniper was suddenly by my ear, yelling, "I'll send pictures."

I hung up before Mom or Dad could answer.

Juniper held out her hand. "Now turn off the phone and give it."

That was when I hesitated. Not for very long, but Juniper noticed. Part of why my sister was here was to take our valuables and drive the SUV back to the resort she was staying at with her husband.

I'd always known I'd need to hand over my phone, but in the moment it was harder than I'd imagined. It didn't matter that my phone would lose reception and die in the mountains. Most of my life was on my phone. What would I do without it?

But this whole trip was for Brittany. Giving up my phone was one of the ways I'd show Britt how much I cared. I could survive without my phone since I'd be with her.

I carefully shut down my phone before handing it over.

"And your wallet," she said.

"No," I replied instinctively.

My sister scrunched her nose. "You agreed..."

Sure I had.

I know I had.

But in the past Juniper's gone through my wallet and *borrowed* cash.

Beside me, Paul handed over his phone, wallet, and a massive ring of keys. "Thank you," she said with a pointed look in my direction.

I gave Juniper my wallet right as a two-door sports car came roaring into the parking lot, its tires squealing as it parked. Three guys emerged. They were post-college. One of them was maybe a year or two older, but they all had strong *bro*-energy.

If I heard correctly—and they were talking loudly enough that half the mountain must've heard—they were debating protein powders.

"Stop staring," Juniper whispered, but she also couldn't look away. They were just too obnoxious.

The bros removed backpacks from the sports car's tiny trunk. The oldest one was ready to head for the trail when one of his buddies called, "Wait. We have a gift in honor of your upcoming sentence—I mean wedding." The guy laughed way too hard at his own joke.

The third guy tossed a bro-tank. When the oldest unfolded it, he revealed the text across its front: *doomed 4 ∞*.

I rolled my eyes. Anyone who chose the infinity symbol over writing the word *infinity* must be flexing a pseudo-fancy education.

If there'd been any question of this group being a bachelor party, the o's in *doomed* were two wedding rings.

"Doomed for infinity?" Paul groaned. "They're going to Infinity Falls."

"Huh?"

"The waterfall we're hiking to makes the shape of a sideways infinity symbol."

A sideways infinity symbol?

"Isn't that a number *eight*?"

Juniper snorted. "Way to take the romance out of it."

I gave my sister an unimpressed glare. We were in the Idaho wilderness, where the amenities included no running water—hard to be romantic when you stink.

If the bro-tank wasn't enough, one of them shouted, "Final days of freedom!" as they headed for the trail.

Paul cracked his neck, and his eyes were flaming. He checked the public bathroom Sienna had gone into before brushing a hand against the side pocket of his shorts.

Wait.

Paul was annoyed by a dumb comment some preppy post-college bro had made?

What had the guy said? Something about marriage being the pits. Then Paul had looked for his girlfriend and checked his pants pocket. Was he planning a proposal? And was he carrying the ring in an outside pocket of a pair of hiking shorts?

"Is something wrong?" Paul asked.

I shook my head. "Nope, I'm good." I tried to do the math. Paul had been in jail for a crime he hadn't committed for around two years. He'd been released for one year. I couldn't remember how long they'd been dating before his wrongful arrest. However long, he must be getting ready to propose.

"You're right." Paul's voice was quiet. "That's why we're here. Now, be cool."

I wasn't surprised that Paul was planning on marriage. But hiking? Who wanted to get engaged while covered in grime?

"What happened?" Brittany asked. Who knows what my face was doing, but my girlfriend had appeared and was worried about me.

"Nothing," I said.

Britt cupped my jaw, which was rough from not shaving this morning.

Frequently, I'll rock sexy-scruff on vacation. And on a trip where I was limited to only one change of underwear, I didn't bother with a razor.

Britt frowned, outlining a tiny scar by her eyebrow. "You're sure nothing's wrong?"

Did she know about Paul's plan to propose?

Before I could find a subtle way to ask, Sienna arrived. With Sienna present, the upcoming proposal couldn't be referenced.

Thankfully, my sister was keeping quiet, though her eyes were bright with excitement. It's a wonder Juniper hadn't sniffed out the diamond ring earlier. Not that anything Paul picked would compare to the massive rock that weighed down her hand.

"We ready?" Sienna asked.

"Yeah," Paul said. He bent down and picked up his girlfriend's backpack and held it for her, like he was an old-timey gentleman helping a lady with her coat.

Sienna was short. Her dreadlocks piled on top of her head added a good three inches, but she still barely reached Paul's chin. Once the pack was situated, Paul whispered in her ear, and Sienna brushed her hand against Paul's chest, over his heart.

Huh. Should I be cuter? In the past my sister has accused me of not being romantic.

I picked up Britt's backpack and tried to be chivalrous, but backpacking-backpacks are an odd size and squishy in unexpected places. It ended up being more work for Brittany to wriggle it on with my help than if she'd done it by herself.

Before I could attempt to whisper anything romantic in her ear, Britt had her hand in mine. "You'll do great," she said. "I'm so proud of you."

Luckily, my sunglasses hid the eye roll.

What was with people being proud of me? Did I want to give up my twenty-first-century quality of life to rough it in the woods? No. Absolutely not. But I wanted Brittany to know that I loved her. If that meant my grand romantic gesture involved not showering for days, so be it.

We could have left a full five minutes earlier than we did. The problem was, once our packs were on, Juniper made us wait so she could take an *appropriate* number of group shots. Right after Juniper had given us permission to leave, she threw her arms around me in an impulsive hug.

"Last chance to back out," she whispered.

"Not happening," I said.

"Hm." Juniper squeezed a little tighter. She still couldn't believe I was willingly backpacking. But she let go, then stood by the SUV and watched as the four of us began walking up the trail and gradually disappeared through the trees.

Though I'd put on a brave face, this trip left me feeling *doomed for infinity*.

CHAPTER 2

The day went how you'd expect.

There were trees. There was a path. The four of us walked on the path between the trees. There was no avoiding the dirt and bugs, even when we stopped for breaks.

I don't understand what the big deal is about nature. It's all so...rugged.

For instance, at lunch we stopped at a lovely little trailside clearing. The online reviews didn't do it justice. This charming eatery boasted a rock, large enough to seat all of us, where we dined extravagantly on energy bars and lukewarm water before resuming our trek. With such excellent service, I would've left a large tip, but my sister had my wallet.

I don't know. It's not like the day was awful. But every step forward took me farther away from civilization. The stillness became more pronounced, and the trees crowded closer together.

Britt grew more relaxed as we went, but I grew more on edge. Beyond wild animals, who knew how many bandits and killers were hiding in the mountains.

Once, we met a pair of hikers walking down the trail. They were lucky enough to be returning to flushing toilets. Otherwise, we were completely swallowed by the trees.

There was still plenty of daylight when we got to our campsite. In the center was blackened earth encircled by a ring of rocks—presumably the firepit—with a couple of logs resting around it.

The surrounding area was clear enough for tents to be set up without being too close to their neighbors. Through the trees branched a network of trails. Some were little more than footpaths, while others seemed to get a lot of use.

The three bros from the parking lot had already set up their tent. They may have been annoying, but there was an easy camaraderie among them. Based on their behavior, I'd guess two of them were brothers and the third was a close friend.

Paul and I began pounding in tent stakes when Younger Brother joked, "Last chance to disappear before you're shackled to the missus."

Paul's head snapped up and his hands flexed, but he didn't say anything.

I took a deep breath. How had I managed to get my nose in the middle of my girlfriend's brother's proposal? I'm thirty-one years old. Will there ever be an age when I'll be free from drama?

"Ignore them," I said. "They're idiots."

Paul's eyes twinkled. "Well put."

My attention shifted back to the bros instead of the job of tent building.

"Holt!" Paul's warning came a second too late. My thumb radiated with pain as I accidentally hit my thumb instead of the stake. I grunted from the shock. But it was sore, not broken.

"That must hurt," Paul said. "Why not have Sienna sub in? She's great at pitching tents." Without waiting for me to agree, Paul called, "Sienna."

She came right over. She had a swing in her step even after hours of hiking.

"You're subbing in. Holt smashed his thumb."

Sienna nodded but surprised me by grabbing my hand and moving my thumb around. "You should be fine once the smarting stops."

"Um, thanks," I said—it's not like I'd even asked to stop working on the tent. Sure, under normal circumstances, I would assume he got Sienna to replace me because he wanted to spend time with his girlfriend. But this seemed like Paul was making the most of the opportunity to work with a more experienced tent builder.

Why were my tent-making skills being called into question?

"Holt, why don't you fill up the pot with water from the creek and...uh...get firewood?" Paul kept his focus on the tent as he said it.

We both knew finding firewood was an official demotion. As important as it is for building fires, that's the job traditionally given to children so they stay out of the way.

My jaw twitched, but I accepted my new assignment without an argument.

It's not like I think I'm too good to scrounge around foliage for abandoned branches...but the way Paul hastily maneuvered to get Sienna to help was offensive.

I *can* set up a tent. They're designed to be put together at night during a rainstorm. I'm an engineer. I can figure it out.

But based on Paul's reaction, I'd been messing up the process. I'm not sure how. It's not like I turned the thing inside out.

What I wanted was a real cup of coffee. What I got was a pot of questionable water, followed by marching through underbrush searching for branches. The campsite was popular enough that I wandered a decent way from camp before I was able to find suitable firewood.

As I worked, I kept getting closer to the creek that was near the trail.

I began creating a pile to bring back to camp when the snapping of a twig had me instinctively hiding behind a tree—it was probably a bear.

Voices drifted through the air.

Not a bear...unless the forest had talking bears like in animated movies.

"I just need a little more time." It was a man's voice, but unusually high and pretty desperate.

Peeking around the tree, I could see the friend was talking to Younger Brother. They were farther away than I expected. Their voices really carried in the silence.

"Do you think I like this?" Younger Brother asked. "Do you think I'm glad my brother's best man is a loser who couldn't keep a penny to save his life?"

"You want your money now? Fine. Whatever, Kyle. I'll pay an installment. Oh, but then I won't be able to pay rent and I'll get evicted. Will your brother let me borrow his tent once the trip is over? That way I'll have something to live in."

Younger Brother's voice was emotionless when he answered. "Your little act has grown predictable. What did you say two months ago? You'd have to move into an abandoned dumpster? Comparatively, living in a tent is pretty nice."

"Whatever, Kyle!" And Broke Friend stormed off.

"You'll be fine," Younger Brother called as he followed at a much slower speed. "You conned me. I'm sure you'll find a new mark."

I stood frozen in place after their footsteps had faded away. After what I'd overheard, I would do absolutely anything to avoid them. There was no way I was getting involved in their squabble.

I waited an appropriately long amount of time before I resumed getting branches. As I worked, I replayed their conversation.

My assumption was correct that the group consisted of two brothers, and the older one was getting married. But the friend owing Younger Brother a large sum of money was new. And strange.

Why did Younger Brother pick a desolate spot to argue about money? Was that a conscious choice or something that happened accidentally?

"Holt, where are you?" Brittany's voice brought me back to the present.

"Over here," I called.

It didn't take long for Britt to find me.

"You look handsome," she said, reaching up to kiss me.

My eyebrows shot up. Somehow, I doubted the clothes stained with dried sweat and hair that was flopping into my eyes were attractive.

"Aren't you glad we came?" Britt's face was relaxed, and she seemed truly at peace.

But being at peace made no sense given all the wildlife lurking in the forest. Plus, in any sort of medical emergency, it would take hours for help to arrive, and you'd need to find space in your budget for a helicopter ride.

Brittany took my extended silence as an answer on my thoughts about the wilderness. "I see." A bit of the brightness left her eyes. I guess we were both sad we couldn't equally share this experience.

I winked. "Yay, nature."

"That's the spirit," Britt said. Her attention shifted past me to my collection of firewood. "Wow, you've been busy." She giggled. "We're not planning a bonfire."

"Right," I said, running a hand through my hair—something I instantly regretted when I remembered how grimy my hand was. "It's been a while since I've sung campfire songs. I wasn't sure what we needed."

"This should last."

Together, we shuttled the branches back to the campsite. Older Brother was there doing some form of outdoor supper preparation, but Younger Brother and Broke Friend were missing.

My neck tingled like something bad was about to happen. But whether it was intuition or an overactive imagination, I couldn't tell.

Paul got the fire going and set up a strange sort of tripod, which he hung my pot of water over. Once the water boiled, he poured it into waiting bags of freeze-dried spaghetti and sealed the bags shut. After waiting a few minutes, Paul declared the food was cooked.

When I took my first bite, I fought the urge to gag. Somehow the spaghetti was soupy and crunchy while being too hot.

The food wasn't great, but I was stranded in the mountains with the choice of gross spaghetti or skipping dinner. Under normal circumstances, I wouldn't have eaten, yet this was day one of backpacking, and I needed all the calories I could get.

Another group of four hikers joined our site midway through supper. It was probably a family. A middle-aged man with three young adults. At some point, Younger Brother and Broke Friend returned, having calmed down. Each group kept to itself, except when they needed to use the fire. Not a big deal, but you'd think they could bother to find some firewood...though Britt was right. I had found more than enough firewood to last the night.

I'm not sure what the social protocols are regarding campfires in nature, but our group had earned the right to sit around the fire, while the other campers stayed closer to their tents.

Everyone seemed relaxed and in good spirits. The sun set, and the woods darkened until the main light came from our campfire.

While sitting on an ancient log full of carved initials would never be my first choice, I'd begun to relax. Britt was sitting right beside me, and she was so content I couldn't help but be glad I'd come along.

"Are you ready, Brittany?" Paul asked.

"Ready?" Britt shook her head. "Don't tell me you've planned another scary story?"

Paul winked at his twin. "Come on, sis. We've gotta honor tradition." He was sitting on the ground, resting against a big rock, with Sienna leaning against him. Paul began. "It was on a dark moonless night—"

"Like this one?" I couldn't help asking.

"Precisely," he said, unbothered by my interruption.

Great.

I moved closer to Britt and wrapped my arm around her. In general, I'm not a big fan of scary stories. Why Paul felt the need to tell one in the wilderness was beyond me.

Paul continued speaking, his face flickering from the light of the fire. "Ezekiel Bull was a logger whose hands were so tough his calluses had calluses."

"What happened to the moonless night?" I whispered to Britt.

Britt just shook her head.

"Ezekiel Bull's friends called him loyal, but his enemies called him mean and..." As Paul continued, the other campers stopped their conversations and moved closer to hear Paul's story.

"But Ezekiel wasn't as honorable as his friends would have liked. This big, mean man with calluses on calluses would cheat at cards. To the casual player, it seemed his luck during bunkhouse games would never run out. But in the mountains, at a logging camp, far from civilization, not all the poker players were so trusting."

Paul's eyes searched beyond the fire as though the past were playing out before him. "Higgins was new to the camp. No one knew much about him. He never told anyone he used to be a hangman, but he could always spot a crook. One night he exposed Ezekiel Bull's treachery to the whole camp. Everyone was outraged and pistols were drawn, but Ezekiel had disappeared in the confusion. He left the site riding a horse with nothing but the clothes on his back. The other men chased him, but riding horseback through the woods in the dark became too dangerous. All of them gave up. All but one."

Paul paused dramatically.

"Higgins the hangman," someone murmured in the silence.

"Yes," Paul said. "Hangman Higgins wouldn't give up. Day or night, neither man slept, and they rested their horses only when necessary. Higgins was always close behind, but he could never quite catch Ezekiel Bull."

I whispered to Britt, "Wasn't this supposed to be spooky?"

"Paul's getting there," Britt said.

She'd heard this story? Were Ezekiel Bull and Hangman Higgins part of Asato pop culture? Did Sienna already know what happened?

"Three nights later Ezekiel was leading his horse through an extra-treacherous stretch of mountain. Actually"—Paul paused and twisted toward one of the trails that spiderwebbed out of the campsite—"it must've happened near here."

I 100 percent blame my sudden shiver on an unexpected breeze...It had nothing to do with Paul's story. Obviously, Paul's story would somehow involve these mountains and probably this campsite.

"The horse was barely lifting its feet, too exhausted with the days and nights of fleeing, when disaster struck for Ezekiel. The horse stumbled, lost its footing, and slid down a ravine. The horse cried out in pain, and all Ezekiel could do was put it out of its misery. Ezekiel was left alone in the woods, with Hangman Higgins close behind."

A log snapped in the fire, and I wasn't the only person to jump.

What was with me? It had to be the ambience. No way I'd be this tense if Paul were telling this story in my well-lit apartment.

"Hangman Higgins heard the cries of Ezekiel Bull's horse and knew the time had come to bring another scoundrel to justice."

"Well..." Paul pretended to yawn. He seemed ready to suggest we all call it a night. Britt gave an almost imperceptible shake of the head, and Paul continued.

"In the end Ezekiel Bull wasn't a coward. He wasn't going to hide in a tree and live in fear that Higgins might spot him. He went out to meet Higgins on that dark, moonless night. But"—Paul shook his head—"Ezekiel was crafty. He wasn't going to let Hangman Higgins take him without a fight. It was dark enough that Ezekiel didn't draw his pistol but instead took his long hunting knife and a large rock, then lay in wait."

Strange shadows moved across Paul's face. "Ezekiel had nothing to lose. He was willing to fight to the death."

I'll spare the gruesome details—a courtesy Paul didn't provide us.

Apparently, Paul had been holding back. He got really into the more violent portion of the story. There were sound effects for Higgins being hit by a rock and falling to the ground. What followed was a battle between the card sharp and the hangman, which Paul described blow by blow, all while flames danced eerily around us.

The result of the final showdown was that Ezekiel Bull had stolen the horse, and Hangman Higgins was stranded...Oh, and Higgins had lost one of his hands in the fight. (That was the gory bit.)

"They say Higgins's hand has a life of its own," Paul added ominously. "It crawls around the forest like a five-legged tarantula looking for the rest of Higgins's body." Paul stretched and yawned for real. "Who's ready for bed?"

You've got to be kidding me. Fake or not, the image of a hand crawling across pine needles like a *five-legged tarantula* was burned into my brain.

"There are no tarantulas this far north," Brittany whispered, since my whole body was tense.

I nodded. Maybe that was true, but Britt could be lying to spare my feelings.

Tarantulas.

I'd been too worried about bears to consider that dangerous creatures came in all shapes and sizes.

"Paul's right," Britt said, gently pushing me. "It's time to call it a night."

I got up slowly. Parts of my back and legs were stiff after cooling down from the day's hike. The family of four hikers was also heading to bed, but the boys from the bachelor party were in no hurry.

As we prepared for bed, my attention kept wandering back to the bachelor party. The three of them were laughing and talking loudly. Apparently they were in good spirits. Yet from the argument I'd overheard, there was plenty of drama looming under the surface.

It didn't take long to complete a nighttime routine. All we'd been allowed to pack was a toothbrush, and we shared a communal tube of toothpaste. The most time-consuming part was securing all the food in a bear bag and hanging it in a tree. Then our packs were arranged around a tree near our tent. We did this because...I actually don't know why. Paul said we had to. Apparently, you're just supposed to trust that other hikers won't steal your stuff.

It's also why you leave your wallet at home.

"Hurry, before all the mosquitoes get in," Paul called from inside the tent, since I'd been distracted again by the three guys.

"My bad," I said as I crawled into the tent.

For a moment I couldn't breathe. I'd realized we'd be sharing close quarters, but picturing four grown-ups crammed into a tiny tent was different from seeing four sleeping bags overcrowding a space I couldn't stand straight in.

"Here." Brittany patted the sleeping bag between her and the tent's wall.

Paul had hung a flashlight from the highest point of the tent, and it clearly illuminated my discomfort.

I more or less crawled and scrambled over people to get to my spot, before wriggling into the sleeping bag. It was an extra sleeping bag of Paul's and had a strange scent to it. Likely a mixture of sweat and nature. I cleared my throat and hoped I'd acclimate to the smell.

The other three were chatting, but I lay still, hoping sleep would come quickly.

It didn't.

While I've taken plenty of naps on the ground, somehow knowing I was trapped in the forest with nothing but a thin tarp to protect me from bears, tarantulas, and cut-off hands that moved like tarantulas kept me wide-awake.

Shortly after the lantern was turned off, Paul started snoring. I'm not talking a low rhythmic snore that could fade into white noise, but something loud and irregular that I never got used to. It drowned out all the other sounds of nature and was a megaphone alerting all bears to our exact location.

Once, through all the din, I thought I heard a cry, but it may have been an owl, and Paul was so loud I couldn't trust my ears.

Also, I was getting surprisingly hot. The four of us radiated heat, which became trapped in the space with no airflow. I unzipped the sleeping bag and lay there in my T-shirt, trying to comfortably pillow my head on a sweatshirt since pillows weren't allowed.

Nothing helped. I could feel the three of them beside me. The air was thick with too many people sharing it. Sure, technically Britt was on one side and the tent was on the other, but I felt claustrophobic knowing there were so many people in the small space.

The night wore on, and I still couldn't sleep. I began shifting closer and closer to the edge of the tent until my body was resting against the side. I don't know how late it was when my body began relaxing. My eyelids grew heavy, and my head rolled so it was pressed against the tent's wall.

In this state I was neither awake nor asleep. Visions of Hangman Higgins's hand crawling through the forest played across my mind. Not quite a dream, but almost...

I may have dozed off.

Or I probably dozed off, when—through the fabric of the tent—fingers dragged along my shoulder and across my head.

Hangman Higgins's hand had found me!

Suddenly I was wide-awake and screaming. I jumped up, forgetting how low the ceiling was and half toppled over, doing my best not to crash-land on Britt.

Everyone else woke up—though Britt was the first to form a full sentence. "What's wrong?"

"Hand! The hand. Higgins—I, it..."

In the darkness it sounded like Paul laughed, but by the time Sienna clicked on the lantern, his face was serious.

"All right." Britt placed her hands on my chest. "Try to slow down your breathing. Here. Let's breathe together." The woman talking had transformed from my girlfriend into a full-time paramedic.

I trusted her enough to follow along, and soon the pounding in my heart slowed down. The problem with calming down was that I became aware of the scene I'd caused. "Sorry," I said, staring down at my sleeping bag.

"We all get nightmares," Paul said as he lay back down.

"Yeah, Paul can get a little carried away around campfires," Sienna said. She made it sound like it was one of her favorite things about him.

Britt brushed hair off my forehead. "It's okay to be scared."

For a moment all I could do was stare at them. I surprised everyone by saying, "No."

"You weren't scared?" Britt asked.

"Not that." I shook my head. "It wasn't a dream."

Paul sat up with a grunt. "What wasn't a dream?"

"There were fingers that brushed my shoulder and head."

"Brittany must've shifted and touched you," Sienna said.

"No," I repeated. "The hand was outside the tent."

"Outside?" Paul asked, his eyes flicking past me, clearly skeptical.

"Are you sure?" Britt asked. My girlfriend seemed more concerned about my sanity than any outside threats.

"Yes, I'm sure," I snapped.

From the way Britt, Paul, and Sienna were glancing at each other, no one believed me.

"Maybe a raccoon or squirrel brushed the tent?" Sienna suggested. It was an interesting theory. It was also the closest any of them had come to accepting I wasn't confused about reality.

"Possibly," I said, since I didn't want to lose my one ally—plus, a raccoon was more likely than Hangman Higgins's tarantula hand.

"Shouldn't we...?" I hesitated. "You know, go and check it out?"

Paul blinked sleepily. "Not necessary."

He was staying put? I was supposed to be Paul's backup as he searched for whatever touched me. I didn't want to go by myself.

"All right," I said, pretending like I wasn't freaked out by the thought of investigating alone. I crawled across the sleeping bags until I was at the zipper to the tent flap, where all our shoes were resting.

"Hold on, I'm coming too," Britt said.

"Okay," I said, hoping the dim lighting would hide how relieved I was.

"And me," Sienna said. "Paul?"

He gave a tired smile. "I guess we're all going. Let's go find Hangman Higgins's missing hand."

Once everyone had their shoes on, we left the tent—each of us armed with a flashlight. When we got to the side of the tent where my head had rested, there was...nothing.

Chapter 3

Maybe I was more tired than I'd realized. Even if an actual hand had touched me through the tarp, it was likely whoever the hand belonged to would have left in the time it took from me raising the alarm to all of us tumbling outside.

There was an awkward silence when none of them looked in my direction. None of them believed something had touched my head. It was true I was half-asleep when it happened, yet there was no dreaming the sensation of fingers brushing me through a tent wall.

Could this be a practical joke? Someone from one of the other tents deciding to have some fun at my expense?

I shone my flashlight along the ground. The natural pattern of the scattered pine needles was gone.

"Holt?" Britt asked as I crouched down to get a better look.

"Here," I said. "The ground's been disturbed."

Paul was mid-yawn when I announced my discovery. At first all he did was shake his head, but when he could speak, he said, "Look around." And shone his flashlight across the ground. "Everything's been disturbed from us pitching the tent." His light flashed into the foliage. Had something moved? But the next instant Paul's light was somewhere else. "There's nothing here."

That sentence was all the three of them needed to go back to bed.

"Come on." Britt took my hand. "It's late. You'll feel better in the morning."

With my free hand, I shone the light toward the spot where I thought there'd been movement. There was nothing but trees disappearing past my flashlight's range.

My spine tingled. My subconscious was noticing information that my brain couldn't decipher.

"Holt?"

I shook my head. I didn't like calling it a night, but it was pitch-dark in the wilderness and my three roommates were too tired to investigate. "Sorry," I said, and walked back to the tent with Britt.

We couldn't have been far behind Paul and Sienna, but Paul had already resumed snoring.

"Good night," Sienna said.

"Night," Britt replied, before cupping my cheek in her hand. "I know camping isn't what you're used to. But we really are safe out here. There's nothing to worry about."

I swallowed. Britt didn't believe me. She thought I was a city slicker who started hallucinating after a few hours in the woods. I decided not to argue. Instead, I cracked a smile. "I'm always safe with you."

Britt's eyes sparkled, and she gave me a playful shove. "Get some rest."

Once I was settled in my sleeping bag, Britt turned off the lamp. While it's hard to confidently say when Britt or Sienna fell asleep with how loud Paul was snoring, I soon had the impression I was the only soul awake.

I stared up at the tent's slanted ceiling as, gradually, my eyes became more accustomed to the dark. This time I made sure I wasn't too close to the tent's wall by scooting closer to Brittany's sleeping bag.

What was happening? Could Sienna be right and instead of human fingers, it was the hand of an overly curious squirrel? Had I been awake enough to know the difference?

A crash in the woods had me tensing, but there were no shouts for help.

I took a deep breath. This was going nowhere. I forced my eyes shut and tried to slow my breathing. It was pointless. My senses were on high alert. Any second I expected someone to cut through the tent with a machete…well, maybe not a machete but something dreadful.

With sleep not being an option, I resumed staring at the ceiling and attempted to piece together what my subconscious noticed in the woods.

First, with Paul's light there'd been the flash of movement, but I hadn't seen anything…Maybe it was branches moving as an animal brushed past. What about when I'd shone my light over the area?

I tried to remember the smallest detail. But there was nothing specific. Only lots of pine trees.

Hold on.

I sat up in my excitement.

Trail.

Hadn't there been a trail?

The marks I'd shown Paul around our tent had continued into the forest. Could they be…drag marks? Had I felt a dead person's hand as they'd been dragged away from camp?

I shifted deeper into the tent. Britt stirred when I bumped her.

Britt.

Should I wake her, and the two of us could investigate?

But what would I tell her? Britt thought I was a city boy who dreamed creatures were clawing at him after one weird story. Would she believe they were drag marks? What if I was wrong?

In the silence right before Paul inhaled another snore, there was a howl from a wild animal. My stomach turned. Maybe we should wait until it was light out. Who knew what murderers and beasts were prowling around in the dark.

I got resettled in my sleeping bag and stared up. It wasn't that I was opposed to falling asleep, but I couldn't. My heart was racing, and sweat was forming around my temples.

For some reason, Britt, Paul, and Sienna sleeping peacefully beside me just made my panic worse. I was the only one keeping watch from the hundreds of predators lurking outside.

The minutes passed by, and gradually Paul's snoring was less apparent. All I needed was to wait until morning. Once it was light, I'd check whether my hunch was correct. If there was a dead body, the murderer should be long gone.

Who would the victim be?

The guys from the bachelor party had been arguing, but they'd been enjoying themselves around the fire. I hadn't learned much about the family of hikers. They might all hate each other.

Each one of them was a potential victim.

Was there anything I missed in their interactions? Something about their body language? I couldn't remember.

A yawn surprised me. Was I actually getting sleepy?

But it must've been a fluke, because my heart was still racing and my eyes refused to close.

Gradually the night began getting lighter, though it was slow enough that I didn't notice when it began.

I yawned again and snuggled deeper into my sleeping bag. I hadn't worn a watch, and without my phone I couldn't keep track of time, but in thirty or forty minutes it should be bright enough to check for a dead body...

"Holt, come on. Wake up." It was Britt's voice, right next to my ear.

I grunted and was drifting back to sleep when a cold hand on my forehead had me prying an eye open.

"Morning, sleepyhead."

"No," I muttered.

I felt Britt's soundless laughter. "Holt, you have to get up. I'm trapped."

Trapped? Brittany didn't sound trapped. I forced my eyes fully open. I was still in the tent, wrapped in the sleeping bag, but in the little time I'd been asleep, I'd moved even closer to Britt and wrapped my arm across her sleeping bag.

I tried to roll away, but my sleeping bag's zipper was caught in hers, and the more I moved, the worse it got. This would have been frustrating fully caffeinated, with a full night's sleep. In my current state, I was ready to rip the bags apart or ask Paul to use his knife to cut us out.

Britt had a less violent solution. She got Sienna to overcrowd our personal space, and Sienna was able to get them untangled.

I rolled away, still half-asleep. My eyes had closed when the suspected dead body in the woods hammered into my consciousness. Suddenly, I was wide-awake.

There's no way I'd slept for very long. But in that time the sky was bright enough to be considered day. Paul had left the tent, while Britt and Sienna were ready to leave.

The morning was cool, and I put on the sweatshirt I'd used as a pillow. I got my shoes and followed Britt outside. Paul had a fire going and had the cooking gear out. "Oatmeal will be ready in five minutes. Instant coffee ready in three."

"Sounds good," I said—though instant coffee barely counts as coffee.

The tent with the dad and adult children had a lot of activity. All four of them were alive, fully dressed, and eating energy bars.

But the tent with the three men seemed abandoned.

"Seen anyone?" I asked, tilting my head toward their tent.

Paul shook his head. "No, but it's not surprising. They were up late."

I shuddered, reliving the fingers dragging across my head. Had it been a prank or a dead body?

"Excuse me," I said, and walked in the direction of the drag marks. No one followed, but I hadn't asked for company. They probably assumed I was answering the call of nature.

What was I doing?

While I've seen my fair share of dead bodies, it's not like I'm in the habit of corpse-hunting.

Should I have brought a weapon? Grabbed a knife or a really big stick?

I should be fine. If there was a murdered body, the *murderer* probably wasn't on-site. Unless…How long before scavenging animals came on-site?

I rubbed a hand along my jaw, my chin already scruffy from not shaving. I was having major second thoughts on my solo mission, but I kept moving forward. Strangely, it had actually been easier to spot the markings in the dirt by flashlight. It had something to do with how the shadows hit the ground.

I walked slowly, careful not to miss any discarded objects or clues along the way. Once I wondered whether I saw a smear of blood on pine needles, but I had no way of knowing for sure. And even if it was blood, it might not be human. It's not like I could tell the difference between a human's blood and a raccoon's.

Just to be safe, I stuck a twig in the ground by that spot to mark the area.

The campsite had disappeared in the blend of trees, but voices and the snap of the fire drifted through the air.

How much farther would I have to go? If a body had been moved to prevent discovery, it would only need to be brought far enough that no one getting kindling or answering nature's call would find it.

I began walking even slower.

Why had I done this alone? I could have told Britt I wanted a few minutes alone together. It would have sounded romantic. I didn't need to embarrass myself by admitting my true motives. She'd have no reason to accuse me of making up conspiracies based on one campfire story.

But I'd kind of committed to walking by myself. I couldn't turn back now.

Ahead of me was a large boulder. My stomach gave a sickening flip. While, yes, technically I couldn't actually know there was a corpse on the other side, I *knew* there would be a corpse.

The only question: Was it the groom, the rich younger brother, or the broke friend?

After a moment's hesitation, I walked around the boulder.

CHAPTER 4

Younger Brother lay still. His limbs were bent in strange positions, he wore socks but no shoes, and there was a nasty gash along his forehead.

All I could do was stare.

A dead man had stroked my head last night. Granted, it was through a tarp, but that was traumatizing enough.

My body was numb. As much as I had expected to find a dead body, I couldn't quite believe it.

Was this shock?

He'd been lying here for hours. Should I have done more last night? Gone by myself to search the woods in the dark?

I shivered.

Who knows. If I'd done that, I might be lying dead next to Younger Brother.

And what happened now? Obviously, I'd tell my group. Then what? How long before the police got here? Would Paul be able to propose?

I tried to smooth back my poofy hair.

"Sorry," I murmured to Younger Brother, even though he couldn't hear it. Finally, I turned around and left.

I walked back to camp in a daze. It's a miracle I didn't get lost.

Sienna was the first person to spot me. "There you are." She smiled. "Here, you look ready for coffee."

I took the metal cup, forgetting the coffee was instant until the taste hit my tongue.

"Are you sick?" Britt asked. "Your face is really white."

"He'll be fine after coffee," Paul said, without looking up from his oatmeal.

I shook my head and set the mug down on a mostly flat section of a log. "There's a dead body," I said.

"What?" Britt looked from me to the section of trees I'd walked from. "Are you sure?"

"Yeah." I hadn't checked for a pulse, but the color of Younger Brother's skin and overall stiffness had been obvious indicators.

"How did it happen?" Sienna asked quietly, to keep the other campers from hearing.

"I'm pretty sure he was murdered."

"Where?" Britt asked.

Just then Paul laughed, but he tried to cover it with coughing.

We all stared.

Sienna frowned. "What's funny?"

"Sorry, Holt," he said. "I didn't mean to ruin your fun."

At the mention of my name, Britt and Sienna shifted their focus to me. I raised a shoulder. "Umm...I have no idea what he's talking about."

Paul's forehead wrinkled. "Isn't this payback for last night? I scared you into having a nightmare, and you thought it'd be funny if..." Paul trailed off when he took a good look at my face. From the set of my jaw and the tightness around my eyes, it was clear I wasn't kidding.

I answered Paul, my voice extra low. "I didn't have a nightmare about a dead hand touching me. There was a hand. The hand was

attached to the dead body of the younger brother staying in that tent."
I pointed to the bachelor party tent.

Instantly, Paul was on his feet. "Is it far?"

"Not far," I said.

"Let's go." Paul abandoned the breakfast.

"Hold on," Britt said as she walked to her backpack. "I'm getting
my first aid kit."

I couldn't help my low whistle. "Trust me, this guy is way past first
aid."

"She's getting the satellite phone from the first aid kit," Sienna said.

A satellite phone? This whole trip they'd been carrying a phone and
no one had bothered to tell me?

Once Britt had the red emergency bag, we walked to the spot where
Younger Brother lay motionless. His head wound looked even worse
than I'd remembered.

"Definitely dead," Paul said.

Brittany took the phone out of the bag, and we all waited as it slowly
turned on. Then Britt dialed and waited for the call to connect. "Hello,
my name is Brittany Asato, and I'd like to report a murder."

Brittany was on the phone for a long time. Then Paul got on the
phone and began explaining exact coordinates and landmarks. He
turned to Britt. "They want us to give the phone to the other hikers
so they can be officially notified to stay and get interviewed. Holt and
Sienna will need to stay with the body."

Paul and Britt left, which meant I was alone with Sienna and a dead
man.

"You were right," Sienna said. "A hand stroked your head last
night."

I nodded. While I appreciated Sienna acknowledging it wasn't all
my imagination, it was hard to concentrate on anything beyond the

body. Even facing away from Younger Brother, I couldn't get the image out of my head.

"What do you think happened?" Sienna asked.

I shrugged. "Hard to say." But I couldn't help wondering about the fight I'd overheard between Younger Brother and Broke Friend. Could the motive be as simple as money?

I almost forgot I was supposed to stay with the body. I wanted to jog back to the campsite and see if Broke Friend was in their tent. Had he disappeared into the night?

If I'd just killed someone in the woods, would I make a run for it, or would I go to bed and pretend nothing happened?

"We should have believed you," Sienna said quietly.

"Thanks," I said.

Things would be a lot different if they had. But it's not like this was Sienna's fault. Of anyone, she'd been the most open to the possibility I hadn't been having a nightmare.

In the trees, there was a fluttering of branches as a bird moved. I looked but couldn't see where it came from. Hopefully, it wasn't a scavenger bird. "Will we have to stay here until the authorities arrive?" I asked. Not only was I dreading the possibility of chasing away wild animals, but my temples were beginning to throb from a lack of caffeine.

"Someone will need to keep watch," Sienna said. "But I'm sure Britt or Paul will be back soon."

I nodded.

This dead body would mess up our travel plans. For my part, it wouldn't be too bad to lose a day of hiking with a pack on my back, but what about Paul? He had his engagement planned at a waterfall. If this trip got shortened or canceled, would he still propose?

I leaned back against the boulder as we waited. Sienna followed suit.

One thing I never thought I'd do: stand guard over a dead body so scavengers couldn't eat it.

How many animals were hiding between the trees? How many of them ate decaying corpses?

"Do you think we'll need to scare anything away?" I asked. "Or is our presence enough to keep animals away?"

"Well"—Sienna took a quick peek at the body—"us being here should be enough to scare most of them."

Most? She said *most.* What animals weren't included in *most,* and were they big?

Not to quote *The Wizard of Oz*, but I didn't need to worry about lions or tigers...Bears, on the other hand, would prove troublesome.

There was more flapping in the branches overhead. Were big, mean birds circling, ready to devour the remains? I couldn't tell.

When I looked back down, my eyes caught a flicker of movement that originally seemed black but on second glance was white.

My eyes bulged, and I flattened myself against the boulder.

"What is it?" Sienna whispered, looking all over, trying to spot what had me so worried.

"Skunk. There's a skunk at your ten o'clock." I took a deep breath. "It's coming our way."

Sienna is way more organic, *give back to nature* than I am. Yet she didn't even check whether there was a skunk before she scrambled up the boulder.

I watched her, too surprised to do anything else. Once Sienna was up, she lay down on her stomach and stretched her arm toward me. "Come on."

I didn't need to be asked twice. My ascent was clumsier, but since I'm at least a foot taller, I didn't have as far to go. After I'd made it up safely, we both crouched to watch the animal.

"Do they eat dead things?" I asked.

"I don't know." Sienna shook her head. "But they usually have rabies."

Rabies? Not only was I in danger of being sprayed, but now I had rabies to worry about?

The skunk wasn't moving fast, just sort of plodding along, but it was heading in our general direction.

I swallowed. It was one thing to be tasked with keeping a set of remains safe, but at what cost? Currently, I was risking rabies and the possibility of smelling like skunk for an indefinite period of time. If I got sprayed, I'd need to hike for miles and ride in a car before there was a chance to bathe.

Wait. Was being sprayed worse than contracting rabies?

"Why do skunks spray?" I asked, watching the animal like it was a bomb about to explode.

"Because they feel threatened."

Okay. Okay. Don't threaten the skunk and we'd be safe.

But the animal kept getting closer.

"I think it eats corpses," I whispered. It made sense that skunks ate decomposing matter—it must help them create such a horrible scent.

How did we get the skunk away from the dead body without scaring it enough that it sprayed?

"Hold on," I said.

"What?"

"This is probably stupid, but"—I glanced at Sienna—"will a skunk die after it sprays?"

"That's honeybees," Sienna said. "Skunks are perfectly all right after spraying."

It's not like I really believed they'd immediately die. Still, a guy can dream.

The skunk had made it to our boulder.

"What do we do?" I whispered.

Sienna shook her head.

How did I scare the skunk enough that it left, without threatening it enough that it sprayed?

I looked around. All I found was a pine cone. I picked it up and threw it far enough that there was a rustle of leaves in the distance. The skunk paused but wasn't distracted for very long.

This was bad. We couldn't have the skunk compromising the crime scene. But I also didn't want rabies—I'm not a fan of foaming at the mouth.

"Umm..." My voice was a little louder, and the skunk froze. "Did you see that?" I asked at an almost normal volume.

The skunk lifted its nose and began sniffing.

"Yes, I see that," Sienna overenunciated.

"I don't think our new friend feels safe around humans," I said a little louder.

"Well, we certainly don't feel safe around him," Sienna said.

The skunk turned around but wasn't retreating.

"That's a very good point," I agreed. This had to be one of the weirdest conversations I'd had. Our words didn't matter, only the effect they had on the black-and-white-striped animal.

"So, Holt, how are things with you and Brittany?"

I side-eyed Sienna. *Really?* She chose now to ask, with a dead man on one side of us and a skunk on the other?

The skunk hadn't moved. "We're good," I said loudly. Then I began to analyze Sienna's question. "Why are you asking? Did Britt say something?"

"He's moving!" Sienna practically yelled in my ear as the skunk began retreating.

"Sienna?"

"Hm?"

I was about to re-ask my question when the snap of branches had the skunk scurrying away into the foliage. A moment later Paul and Brittany came into view.

Paul's eyes sparkled as he took in me and Sienna crouched on top of the boulder. "Did I miss something?"

"Only rabies," I grumbled as I slid off the rock. I turned to help Sienna, but Paul was already lifting her down.

Britt held my travel cup. "You forgot this."

My hand trembled as I took the coffee. I drank, ignoring how Britt was observing me with her paramedic face. The coffee was lukewarm and tasted like instant, but I'd barely slept and didn't have other options.

I drained the rest of it without bothering to breathe.

Apparently, everyone was waiting for me to pay attention. Once I'd licked the final drop, Sienna asked, "What did the rangers say?"

"The main thing is to sit tight. They'll be here as soon as they can," Paul said.

"And don't disturb the remains," Britt added.

Did she think we'd be tempted to do a field autopsy? Sienna and I had done our part to keep the body undisturbed.

"How about that family of campers?" I asked. "Were they surprised about the murder?"

Paul hesitated. "Uh, yeah. I guess."

"They were very...reserved," Britt said.

What did that mean?

Sienna tilted her head. "Did they want to get back to civilization? Like, they were upset they couldn't leave the mountain until they spoke to the rangers?"

"That's the thing." Britt snapped her fingers. "They wanted to keep hiking."

My eyebrows shot up. I'm not Mr. Outdoors, but who in their right mind would want to continue a backpacking trip with a killer on the loose?

"Really?" Sienna asked. "That is strange."

"I don't know." Paul fidgeted like he didn't know what to do with his arms. "Infinity Falls is pretty spectacular."

Britt tensed. "You want to keep going?"

Paul said, "Why not?"

Why not? Maybe because nature is disgusting? That's why humans have chosen to live in homes for thousands of years...And what was that other reason? Oh, yeah, there was a crazed killer lurking in the woods.

My stomach twisted.

The waterfall. That stupid waterfall. Paul had waited years to ask Sienna to marry him. Why had he decided it needed to happen at Infinity Falls?

We had a golden opportunity to cut this trip short. Yet it was Paul's proposal. As much as I hated to, I had to agree with Paul.

"We're already here," I said. "Might as well get to the waterfall. I'd like to see what all the fuss is about."

"What?" The shock on Britt's face had me worried she was going to check me for signs of a concussion.

Sienna went up on tippytoes to kiss my cheek. "I knew you would appreciate nature once you spent enough time in it."

"Right." Britt didn't sound convinced.

Sienna ignored Britt's tone. "I agree with Paul and Holt. We should keep going if the rangers let us."

"Sounds like a plan" is what Britt said. Her focus was on me, waiting for me to comment or grimace.

Britt knew me too well. I wouldn't survive her analysis. I bent my head and pretended to double-check the coffee cup—like I expected more coffee had magically appeared.

"How about Holt and I head back to camp?" Britt suggested. "He could use more coffee."

Paul slung an arm around Sienna. "Works for us."

I was mid-yawn, and gave a thumbs-up before walking with Brittany back to the campsite. I was worried she'd start interrogating me, but instead she took my cup and added more hot water from the pot Paul had resting on the rocks by the fire. I tried not to groan as I got a scoopful of instant coffee crystals.

It was odd. I wasn't actually *that tired*. I'd been worried last night about bears and tarantulas. Today's addition of skunks and murderers had me too jumpy to be sleepy. The main reason I drank the coffee was to avoid a caffeine headache.

"How are you doing?" Britt asked.

I raised an eyebrow. Who was asking? Britt the girlfriend or Brittany the paramedic? Either way, the honest answer was that I was doing pretty bad.

Britt was waiting. I gave a partial grin. "I'm as good as can be expected."

She nodded, the little scar by her right eyebrow growing more defined. "I promise, this is my first camping trip with a dead body."

"Lucky me," I muttered.

I sat on one of the logs that formed a semicircle around the fire and took a long drink of the bad coffee. Across from me, the family around their tent was subdued. We were all waiting for law enforcement.

"Was anyone in the bachelor party tent?" I asked.

Britt said, "No, but"—she lowered her voice and leaned in close—"I peeked inside. It looks like the murder site."

I was half standing when I remembered I'm not actually a member of the police force. I'm not authorized to investigate crime scenes. I sat back down.

"Was there blood in the tent?" I asked. "Why do you think the brother was killed there?"

"First off, if the body was dragged past our tent. The murder must've happened nearby."

"Right." I took another drink.

"And everything was a mess inside. Like the sleeping bags were in heaps. One was inside out. There could have been blood on the sleeping bags, but the fabric was too dark to know for sure."

"Gotcha." I began pacing.

When we'd gone to bed, the three of them had appeared to be enjoying the bachelor party. During the day, Younger Brother had argued with Broke Friend about money. Sometime in the night, Younger Brother had likely been killed in his tent and dragged into the forest. This morning both Older Brother and Broke Friend were missing.

Had Older Brother and Broke Friend killed him together? Or was one or both of them also dead, with their bodies hidden beneath the trees? Should we look for more corpses?

I scanned the area around their tent. What did I expect? An arrow pointing to another dead body?

As I looked, my attention quickly moved past the tree where the bachelor bros had rested their backpacks. Some of the dirt and pine needles around their tent were disturbed. Yet as Paul pointed out last night, it might have happened from setting up camp.

My eyes shifted back to the tree with the backpacks. Something was wrong...but what? I took a couple of steps toward the tree.

Britt noticed.

She followed my gaze and gasped. "A backpack's missing."

Huh. Yeah.

That's what was wrong. Instead of three backpacks resting under the tree, there were only two.

I blame not being able to count to three on the lack of quality caffeine—or shock from finding a dead body. Whichever makes me sound less stupid.

Older Brother and Broke Friend were both missing. Had one of them left with their backpack, or had a pack been stolen?

"How long before the police arrive?" I asked.

Britt shook her head. "Maybe three hours, and that's the absolute minimum."

Right. I knew it would take some time for the police. But were we really supposed to babysit a corpse while the killers escaped?

And what about Paul? Would this ruin his engagement plans?

Britt crouched by the firepit, pouring hot water into a metal mug. She leaned against one of the gray rocks surrounding the fire. Lodged deeply in the ground, the stone didn't shift.

The neighboring dark gray rock didn't look as secure. I bent to get a closer view. The dirt and ash around that rock had been disturbed.

Younger Brother had died from a blow to the head. Had he been hit with a rock from the campfire?

"Can I borrow your flashlight?" I asked.

Britt immediately handed it over.

I shone the light on the rock. We both gave it a close inspection, being careful not to disturb it.

"Here." Britt pointed. "That might be blood."

She was right. A darker stain was present.

I shuddered. The killer using a rock from the firepit and putting it back was pretty creepy. One more reason to hate the woods.

Britt took her flashlight back. "We'll tell the police when they get here." Her voice was trending toward supportive paramedic.

Maybe she was right to be concerned about me. But I cared less about my mental health and more about catching a killer. I kicked at another rock in the firepit. It didn't budge. Based on the size, the rock wouldn't be too heavy.

"What are you doing?" Britt asked.

"Just a hunch," I said.

"And?" Britt prompted when I didn't give more of an explanation.

I shrugged. "These rocks are secure in their spots. It wouldn't be easy to pick one up in the heat of the moment."

Britt frowned. "You're thinking the murder was premeditated."

"Seems likely."

My attention shifted back to the tree with the bachelor bros' missing backpack. I didn't notice Britt had moved until she stood in front of me.

"Here, have some oatmeal." She held out the metal cup with a spoon.

Oatmeal...really?

I try to eat healthy. But there's eating healthy and there's eating prepackaged oats, with three chunks of freeze-dried strawberries.

It was a tricky situation. If I declined breakfast, Britt would either get super worried and start checking for signs of shock or make me eat the oatmeal while explaining how many calories I was burning as I backpacked.

I took the cup, sat on the log, and began swallowing mouthfuls of oatmeal that was too watery.

The family of campers had formed a little circle by their tent. The three young adults were sitting on the ground, while the dad stood and spoke to them in hushed tones.

I guess they were suspects. Really, we were all suspects. Short of a stranger lurking behind the trees, the only people who could have killed Younger Brother were the bachelor bros, the family group, and us.

Was there a way I could get some background information on the other group without interfering with a police matter?

Ordinarily, I'd get my sister Juniper to do the interrogating. Since she wasn't here, I'd have to figure it out by myself.

Britt sat beside me. I jumped, and a spoonful of oatmeal glopped onto the dirt.

"Sorry," Britt said, rubbing my back. "I didn't mean to startle you."

"Uh-huh." My attention wandered back to the other group of campers. "Do you know anything about them?"

Britt's hand stilled. "They have money."

That caught my attention. I twisted to face her better. "How do you know?"

"Look at them," she said. "All their clothes and equipment are name brand and look new. That takes money."

"Or debt."

"True." Britt's eyes sparkled, and she bumped me with her shoulder.

I checked the family's gear. I didn't have the eye for name-brand camping equipment, but none of the gear showed wear or grime.

"They have money," I agreed.

This time it was Britt who said, "Or they want to give the impression of having it."

Younger Brother and Broke Friend had been arguing about money. This family had money. Were they somehow involved?

"They're also inexperienced," Britt added. "See that navy backpack? They could have bought a pack for half the price that would've lasted longer and not caused neck pain."

I couldn't help giving Britt's forehead a quick kiss. "You're, like, pretty impressive."

Britt tried to frown. "It took you this long to figure that out?"

I couldn't help my warm laugh. If it were possible, I loved Britt even more than usual. The problem was I'd laughed loud enough the family heard. They were glaring...and judging.

My jaw tightened. Yes, laughing right after a man's been murdered is inappropriate. But it's not like I'd been laughing about the dead man.

They needed to lighten up.

CHAPTER 5

Maybe my laughter was more offensive than I'd originally assumed. The dad walked over to where Britt and I sat.

Hiker Dad broadened his shoulders. "What's funny?"

Whoa.

That was confrontational.

Was I about to get into a fight?

With the right pair of shoes, Hiker Dad was maybe six feet tall. I set my oatmeal down and stood to my full six one height—more like six two while wearing shoes. "My girlfriend just reminded me how smart she is." I held my hands open in the *I don't want trouble* way. "Sorry if I offended you."

"We're good," he said. "Thanks for clearing that up." He lowered his voice so the young people couldn't hear. "You both saw the body? Was it an accident?"

"Uhh..." I frowned. Wasn't that the sort of question the police should handle?

Brittany was more prepared. She said, "We're not qualified to comment."

"Sure, right." Hiker Dad shook his head. "It's just, we're on a tight schedule. We all took time off to be here. I don't know when we could do this again."

I glanced at Britt. She'd been right. Hiker Dad was more concerned about getting to the waterfall than the dead body.

True, Paul was in a similar boat, but he was going to propose. What reason could Hiker Dad possibly have?

Hiker Dad started to leave, then turned back. "Only, I heard something last night, and if it *was* murder, it might be important."

Oh no.

He'd heard me screaming.

I covered my face with my hand, too embarrassed to answer.

Britt said, "It was probably Holt waking us up when..." She stopped herself from mentioning the dead hand caressing my face. "When we thought Holt was having a bad dream."

Hiker Dad shook his head. "Not then."

"How do you know it wasn't me?"

I ignored Hiker Dad's lips twitching. "Weren't you yelling about Hangman Higgins?"

Heat flooded my face. "Yes, I was."

"That's what I thought," Hiker Dad said. "I heard an argument before that."

Before? I'd been mostly awake leading up to my real-life nightmare. But Hiker Dad's tent was closer to the bachelor party's tent. Plus, Paul's snoring had drowned out most of the outside noise.

"What was the fight about?" I asked.

Hiker Dad nodded toward the trees. "Let's stretch our legs." Britt and I followed him a little ways into the woods. "Look, it could be nothing," he said so quietly, Britt and I had to lean in to hear. "But something bad happened in that other tent. When we went to bed, those guys were acting like buddies, but later one of them got all upset and started yelling that he was walking back."

"In the dark?" Britt asked.

"Affirmative," Hiker Dad said. "The other guys tried to talk him out of it, but his mind was made up."

"How dangerous is that?" I asked Britt.

"It depends," she said. "If he had a good headlamp, the trail is pretty straightforward. Still, thousands of people get lost in the woods every year, and some of them—" Britt cut off before saying the word *die*.

We knew what she meant.

"Did you hear why he was upset?" I asked.

The guy shook his head. "No idea. But whoever was leaving sure sounded mad."

I nodded. "Thanks."

But what was I supposed to do with that information?

Hiker Dad didn't even know which man was trying to leave in the middle of the night. Was it the murder victim or a different bachelor bro?

Overhead, a screeching bird had me jumping.

Britt's lip quirked, but she didn't laugh. Nature was bad enough without the dead body.

"Can we check with your family to see if they heard anything?" Britt asked.

Hiker Dad raised one shoulder. "If they don't mind, I don't mind."

When the three of us walked to the hiker family's campsite, Hiker Dad's daughter asked, "What were you all whispering about?"

The question had been a challenge, but I ignored her tone and said, "We were talking about voices in the night. Did you hear anything?"

The woman shrugged like the question was both boring and beneath her. "I woke up to someone screaming about that hangman. Dad said that was you."

"I...uhh"—I raked a hand through my hair—"I meant earlier. Did you hear any yells or maybe an argument?"

"No." Uptight Daughter crossed her arms. "I didn't hear anything. I didn't see anything. And I couldn't have killed anyone since I was sharing a tent with three other people." She stood up. "Now, if you'll excuse me, I need to purify drinking water at the creek."

Wow.

Why had Uptight Daughter been so difficult? First she'd challenged me, then rushed to give an alibi. It was definitely suspicious.

But I couldn't let that distract me. I needed to talk with Hiker Dad's son and *hopefully* the son's girlfriend...I never rested my hand that high on either of my sisters' legs.

The guy was young, and his hair was done in a way that his future self would be embarrassed about and call a *phase*. The girlfriend had aqua-colored hair. She was attractive in a slightly edgy way.

"Did either of you interact with the men staying in that tent?" I asked.

They both shook their heads and wouldn't even look at me. They weren't being hostile. Were they scared?

I started to ask, "After you went to bed—" but I was interrupted.

"None of this is any of your business," said Hiker Girlfriend.

"Yeah, just leave us alone," Hiker Son added.

"Right," I said. "Sorry."

I looked at Brittany and shrugged. We walked back to our place by the fire.

The actual interviews would need to be left for the police. While we hadn't gained new information on the bachelor bros, we'd learned this family was secretive and easily offended.

"What's going on with them?" I asked in a low voice.

Brittany shook her head. "Maybe they're in shock."

I raised an eyebrow. "You didn't find them extra...I don't know, *weird*?"

Britt's eyes sparkled, but she didn't smile. "It was a *unique* reaction," she admitted. "But being secretive doesn't mean you're a murderer."

"I know," I said. "But if they're not a merry group of murderers, they must be doing something illegal. Maybe smuggling endangered species."

Britt snorted. "Definitely. Their backpacks must be full of cages for trapping squirrels."

Were squirrels endangered? Britt was probably kidding, but I'd need to double-check once I could use Google again.

I glanced to where Hiker Dad was speaking with the younger two—Uptight Daughter was still by the creek.

Hiker Girlfriend was rubbing Hiker Son's back as he hunched over, with his head in his hands. Hiker Dad sat on the other side of his son and was talking. The whole scene was intimate, something that usually happened in a house behind closed doors.

I shouldn't stare, but my eyes wandered back to the little group, just as Hiker Girlfriend pressed a kiss on Hiker Son's shoulder.

I shuddered. I really hope that's his girlfriend.

As the older man talked, his hand moved and a band glinted on his ring finger.

"Where's the mom?" I asked.

Britt wrapped her arm around me. "Not everyone's as outdoorsy as we are."

"Sure."

Maybe the mom's absence wasn't important. I wasn't outdoorsy. And in a world where I'd been with Britt long enough to have two adult children, I'd be doing my best to stay home in peace and quiet while Britt went camping with the kids.

Still, there was something off with that group, and the most obvious possibility was the missing mother.

Hiker Dad's kids were likely early twenties. Definitely post high school, yet young enough that they didn't resemble my peers. The dad was maybe fifty. His face bore wrinkles from frequent smiling, but he looked exhausted.

Then again, it was hard not to be tired when you were sleeping unprotected in nature.

I was tired enough to keep staring at their camp until they noticed. I needed a distraction. "Should we take down our tent?"

"Well..." Britt frowned. "I don't know what the police will want to see."

"But I could repack the sleeping bags?"

"Might as well."

Once I was in the tent, I momentarily considered taking a nap instead. I'd feel safer sleeping in the daylight when other people were awake. Besides, who knew how long it would be before the cops showed up?

But Paul had his proposal. We needed enough time to hike to Infinity Falls. If that meant I spent my time making sure our backpacks were ready, that's what I'd do.

Once I'd bagged all the sleeping bags, I carried them out to the tree where our backpacks were resting. I had just clipped Britt's sleeping bag into place when she snuck up behind me.

"Hey," she said. "Are you doing all right? You seem a little off."

Off?

I ran a hand through my hair. I was about twenty-four hours into a technology detox. And not only was I unable to enjoy the benefits of indoor plumbing, but I'd also been forced not to pack any hair product, and my hair was becoming uncontrollably poofy...and the whole *dead body* thing.

Under the circumstances, I was handling the trip rather well.

"You know me"—I tried not to grimace—"I'll always find something to complain about."

I was about to attach my sleeping bag when I noticed an outside zipper was open. Weird. Under normal circumstances, I always triple-check my zippers. Imagine how much more paranoid I am in the wilderness.

"What's wrong?" Britt asked, catching my frown.

"I'm sure I closed this," I said. "Do raccoons open zippers?"

"Well...it's possible," Britt said. She moved right beside me and stared down at my pack. "Was there food inside?"

I shook my head. For all the speeches and warnings Paul had given about proper food storage, I'd made sure not to leave a single bread crumb in my pack.

"Was anything taken?" Britt asked.

I felt around in the pocket and came up empty. Problem was, I didn't remember what was supposed to be there.

"Let me see," I said, checking other pockets. They were all shut, yet not quite all the way. Something or someone had gotten into my bag in the middle of the night.

"Hold on," I said, remembering. "My knife. The knife Paul got me is missing."

"Okay." Some of the color left Britt's face, but she remained calm. "Did you leave it somewhere?"

I was shaking my head even before Britt finished asking the question. "No. I haven't used it." I brushed grime off my shirt, suddenly feeling like a ridiculous city slicker. "I haven't had a reason to use the knife."

Could my knife be the murder weapon? Had it killed Younger Brother?

From what I'd noticed, he'd died from a blow to the head with a blunt object. Meaning the murder weapon was likely the rock from the firepit. But I hadn't gotten close to the body. Could he have been stabbed?

"You saw the brother," I said quietly. "That head wound, was it from a knife?"

Britt paused, the tiny scar by her eyebrow growing more defined as she concentrated. Finally, she shook her head. "I'm not a medical examiner. But I don't think so."

"Good." I exhaled a breath I hadn't realized I'd been holding.

"You're sure the knife's missing?" Britt asked.

I nodded. "Positive."

"Why would anyone take it?" Britt asked. "We're backpacking. I'd bet every person out here has at least one knife."

"Good point," I said—though why would *every person* need their own knife? Twenty-four hours into camping and I hadn't needed a knife.

Britt asked, "Was anything else taken?"

I shook my head. "Not that I can tell."

"Well, that's good, I guess," Britt said, but she was frowning down at my backpack—probably still mystified why anyone would steal my knife. "Do you think the killer has it?"

"Nope," I said. "The killer wouldn't want the attention that came from carrying stolen property."

"True," Britt said. "Why would someone else take it?"

I shrugged. "Protection?"

"I guess so," Britt said. "But we've been around our packs all morning. No one could have taken it after we found the body. What was the person needing protection from?"

"Bears," I said. "Always bears."

Also, this morning there were two times we'd all left the campsite. Once when I showed them the body and when Britt and Paul were saving us from the skunk. Not only could the theft have happened during either of those times, but there was no telling who might have prowled in my pack during the night.

"Maybe Paul or Sienna borrowed it," Britt suggested—though she didn't sound convinced.

"Sure," I said. But I didn't like it. My knife coming up missing was unfortunate.

Overhead, a noise began coming through the trees that was so normal at first I didn't notice. It was only when the thrumming grew louder that I realized the sound of aircraft was out of place in the mountains.

"They sent a helicopter?" I asked.

Britt raised her eyebrows. "It appears so."

The noise grew louder until it was hard to think. Finally, the helicopter hovered above our clearing.

The helicopter's door swung open, and two backpacks were lowered to the ground. Next came a rope ladder and a man who climbed down it easily. A second man's head appeared through the door, but he hesitated. Presumably, he was calculating the risks of climbing down a rope ladder that was suspended in the sky by a flying object.

The man who was waiting on the ground waved his arm, gesturing for his friend to join him.

The head disappeared, and I expected the ladder to be pulled up. Instead, a pair of boots appeared and carefully found the first rungs.

Britt made a comment, but the whirring was too loud. The only word I caught was *bravery*.

We watched as the second man slowly descended the ladder. Halfway down, his hands began shaking. His grip loosened, and he was terrifyingly close to falling. His friend yelled something that was drowned out by the helicopter's blades. But the guy must've heard because he refocused and climbed down safely.

Everyone in the camp relaxed once the second man was on the ground. It was only then that I realized I'd taken Britt's hand and was squeezing it. I let go before wiping my sweaty palm off on my pants.

The ladder disappeared into the helicopter, the door slid shut, and it flew away. The noise soon became a background thrumming—a sound easy to talk over.

The second man still wore his helmet. He was bent over, and it was still too loud to hear him dry heaving.

The first man had removed his helmet and goggles to reveal dark hair and brooding, almost angry eyes. He was probably my age, maybe a little younger.

I was still watching the first man, when the second man straightened and looked right at me.

Then a voice I almost recognized said, "Holt Jacobs?"

CHAPTER 6

H *olt Jacobs?*

How did that guy know who I was? We had to know each other, but with the helmet and the goggles, I couldn't place him.

"Britt?" I murmured, but she shook her head, equally stumped.

Finally, I said, "Yeah, I'm Holt."

"Let me guess," the guy in goggles said. "You don't remember me?"

My head snapped up. That voice with its laid-back sarcasm belonged to someone I'd met...

"Hold on," I said.

"Getting there." The guy sounded amused, but when he tried to move, he clutched his stomach and groaned.

"Hagen, you all right?" the other man asked.

Hagen? Did I know a Hagen?

"From the winery," Britt said right as I snapped my fingers and shouted, "Cop Kid!" My eyes went wide. Why had I used his private nickname?

"Is that how you remember me?" Cop Kid's mouth was a unique combination of smile and grimace.

"You should sit down," his friend with the brooding eyes said.

Hagen nodded and took a step forward. This time he didn't groan, but his jaw clenched and his face turned an impossible shade of white.

Britt was instantly at Cop Kid's side, and with the help of the other man, Cop Kid was brought to a seat on a log. Britt crouched in front of him and undid the helmet strap under his chin. She would have removed the helmet, but Cop Kid held up his hand. "I got this."

He did eventually get the helmet off, but it took multiple tries for his grip to be strong enough to pull it off. He got the goggles off first try.

Even with his face ghastly pale, he looked as young and boyish as I remembered. It was hard to believe Cop Kid was actually older than me.

"What's wrong?" Hagen's dark-haired friend asked. "Are you sick?"

"No, I just..." Cop Kid gestured to the sky that minutes ago held a helicopter with a ladder hanging precariously down to the ground. His friend didn't flinch, apparently clueless to the peril they'd been in. Cop Kid shook his head. "It's motion sickness."

"You're sure?" his friend asked.

"Positive." Cop Kid waved a dismissive hand. "Now, enough about me. Holt and Brittany, meet my cousin, Ranger Jackson Thorne."

The ranger nodded his hello.

Cop Kid was about to continue speaking when Hiker Dad appeared. "Is he all right?"

The ranger nodded. "Hagen will be fine." He looked past Hiker Dad to where the others waited. "You're the family that camped overnight?"

"Yes. We're the Caffreys." Hiker Dad stood a little taller. "Those are my kids and my son's girlfriend."

My throat made a sound at finally confirming the girl with the aqua hair was the girlfriend—thankfully, no one heard.

"Good to meet you." The ranger shook Hiker Dad's hand. "Thanks for sticking around. We'll interview your family once we process the crime scene."

"Yes, sir," Hiker Dad said and rejoined his kids.

The *sir* was a little much. Hiker Dad had to be at least twenty years older than the ranger, but it didn't seem like anyone else noticed.

Cop Kid wiped sweat off his brow before finishing the introductions. "Thorne, this is Holt Jacobs. Don't be offended when Holt doesn't remember your name." He winked at me. "And Brittany Asato, she's a paramedic. I met them during the homicide at Rose's Vineyard." Hagen raised his chin. "Brittany, would you show Thorne where the body is?"

Britt and the ranger opened their mouths, ready to argue. But Hagen was fine. All he needed was a chance to catch his breath without people hovering over him. "That's a good idea," I jumped in. "Britt knows exactly where the body is. I'm sure Paul and Sienna are expecting police after the helicopter."

Ranger Trees, or Thistles, or whatever his name was, frowned. "Hagen, are you sure?"

Cop Kid sighed. "Thorne, I'm positive."

Still, he hesitated a few more seconds before Britt said, "It's this way," and Ranger Trees followed her out of the campsite.

"They gone?" Cop Kid Hagen asked. His back was to them, and he wasn't in good enough condition to turn around and check.

I nodded.

"Good." Hagen sighed. "I thought they'd never leave."

He began sliding off the log. I rushed to catch him, but Hagen raised his hand. "Let me." In a few seconds he was sitting in the dirt and pine needles with his back resting against the log.

Cop Kid stared across the clearing to where their supplies rested. "What do you need?" I asked.

"Water."

There was a water bottle in each backpack. Since I didn't know which one belonged to Hagen, I grabbed both bottles. When I returned, Cop Kid pointed to the bottle in my left hand. "That one."

Hagen was able to hold the bottle, but his hand was shaking too much to press the button that would unlock the lid.

"Here." I took it back, released the lid, and returned it to him.

"I would've figured it out," Hagen grumbled.

I rolled my eyes. "You're welcome."

Cop Kid smirked before taking a long drink.

"Why would you agree to ride in a helicopter if you're afraid of heights?" I asked.

Hagen shook his head. "They were planning on landing the helicopter. Unfortunately, there weren't any good options. And"—a glimmer of humor returned to his eyes—"I wasn't afraid of heights until I was hanging outside the helicopter."

That seemed to track. "But how are you here? Isn't this a little ways out of your jurisdiction?"

"Strange." Cop Kid's voice held barely contained laughter. "I was just about to ask how you ended up caught in another murder investigation."

I glared at him but didn't answer. Cop Kid had almost arrested me for murder when we'd met at the winery. Everything had worked out, but I didn't want him getting any ideas about this putting me behind bars.

I'd stayed silent, but he read my mind. When Hagen spoke, he tried to sound offended but was too laid-back to pull it off. "Did I *actually* arrest you? Did you spend a night in jail?" When I didn't reply, he shrugged. "To answer your question, I'm on vacation."

"Vacation?"

He wiped a bead of sweat off his forehead. "I was spending a week with my cousin, who happens to be a forest ranger. He got called for your dead body, and I tagged along. Though"—Hagen wiped a bead of sweat off his forehead—"maybe I should have waited at his place."

"But then you'd be missing out on your second chance to arrest me for murder."

Hagen's eyes crinkled. "I don't actually have jurisdiction here. It'd be Thorne doing the arresting."

"Too bad," I said. "This was your chance."

Cop Kid sat up. "Are you actually the killer this time?"

I winked.

"If you're the killer, you can tell me," Hagen said. "As a volunteer, I can't make an arrest."

"You could make a citizen's arrest."

Cop Kid laughed. "Those arrests rarely make it to court."

"Too bad," I said. "Better luck arresting me next time."

"Fingers crossed it's in my jurisdiction," Hagen said. "Now"—his face was almost serious—"can you bring me to the crime scene?" He held his hand up, and I helped haul him to his feet.

It wasn't far, yet we walked slowly. Hagen was unsteady on his feet. Once he hiccuped and seemed dangerously close to puking. Thankfully, the moment passed, and we resumed walking.

When we got to the crime scene, Ranger Trees was examining the body, while Britt, Paul, and Sienna all waited on the opposite side of the rock.

Hagen's easy smile appeared when he saw Paul and Sienna. "You're here too?" He shook their hands. "The only person you're missing is—"

"Juniper," I interrupted. "Yeah, my sister isn't big on roughing it."

Cop Kid couldn't quite sound serious as he asked, "And you enjoy *roughing it*?"

He'd got me there. My hair was a poofy mess, and I was covered in dust and dried sweat, with no chance to shower. I wrapped an arm around Britt. "I like making my girlfriend happy."

Cop Kid grinned. "Smart man,"

That ranger guy must've heard our voices because he appeared from the other side of the boulder. "Holt, you're the one who found the body?" His dark eyes were unusually intense.

I nodded.

"And why were you this far from camp?" he asked.

I glanced at Cop Kid. Was Ranger Trees about to blame me for this death?

When I didn't reply, the ranger added, "Were you answering the call of nature?"

Heat rushed up my face. "No. Uhh..." I took a deep breath. "I suspected something bad happened last night."

Ranger Trees's jaw tensed. "And you waited until this morning to check?"

"Well, I tried to yesterday, but..." I realized I couldn't finish the sentence without admitting my friends hadn't been concerned.

"We told Holt he'd had a nightmare," Britt jumped in.

"I'd told a scary story around the campfire," Paul added.

"Understood." Ranger Trees's intense eyes rested on Paul, then flicked to his cousin Hagen, before he asked me, "How many people were camping with the victim?"

"Two," I answered. "It was the victim's older brother's bachelor party. There was also a friend along."

"Where are these men now?" Ranger Trees asked.

"Missing," I said.

"Hm." A frown practically shadowed the ranger's entire face. "Has anyone seen either man this morning?"

We shook our heads.

"There was a fight," Britt said. "One of them left early in the night."

"To walk down the mountain?" A new emotion crept into the ranger's voice. It was almost like fear.

"Would you hike this in the dark?" Cop Kid asked his cousin.

The ranger shook his head. "I'd need a very good reason. The trail is clear enough in the light. But downhill, in the dark, you could mistake a deer trail for the path and get totally lost in seconds."

"Whoever left must've had a good reason," Cop Kid commented.

Or was really dumb...

"Anderson's team is already on the trail," Ranger Trees said. "I'll radio her to keep a lookout for our missing hikers."

"Do you think they'll find them?" Sienna asked.

The ranger raised one shoulder, while Cop Kid said, "That depends on whether they want to be found."

"All right," Ranger Trees said. "You all can go back to the campsite. We'll be there soon."

"Can we take down our tent?" Britt asked.

"Uh...yeah," the ranger said. "Should be fine. Just don't leave." He turned to Cop Kid. "Hagen, you good to help out here?"

Hagen's color was still bad, but he raised an offended eyebrow. "Of course I'm good."

"Great." The ranger's words were spoken more to himself, his brain clearly on the next portion of the investigation. "Once we've photographed and logged the scene, we'll prepare the remains for transport and call in the helicopter. We'll do interviews when we're finished."

The other three left, but a monstrous yawn stalled my progress. I overheard Cop Kid ask, "What do you think?"

Ranger Trees grunted. "About the cause of death? Or how prime suspects in one of your homicides showed up near another dead body in Idaho?"

A bird call had the pair looking up and noticing me.

"Sorry..." I tried to come up with an excuse. "Uh, but for cause of death, the killer may have used a rock from the firepit."

"You know where the rock is?" Ranger Trees clarified.

I nodded.

"Show me."

On the way, I spotted the twig I'd placed to mark the possible blood on the pine needles. "Hold on." I crouched low. "When I was following the trail to the body, I saw this."

Ranger Trees took a photo before putting on latex gloves and carefully scooping pine needles and soil into an evidence bag.

Once we returned to the campsite, Ranger Trees followed a similar procedure around the firepit. He knelt by the rock and took a few photos before easing the rock into a large evidence bag. "We'll send these with the body when the helicopter returns."

With that he picked up the probable murder weapon and returned to the murder site.

After he'd left, Britt asked, "Shouldn't Ranger Thorne be more interested in finding the missing hikers?"

"Yeah," I said. "One of them is probably the killer."

Paul shrugged. "For now their priority must be preserving the body."

I nodded.

Don't get me wrong, it's not like I would want my decaying corpse eaten by scavengers, but if this were a game of would you rather, I'd choose my killer getting caught—even if it meant becoming buzzard food.

Paul clapped his hands together. "Let's get packing."

"Give me a sec." Britt walked over to the family and explained that we were allowed to pack up but had to wait for interviews. By the time she returned, Paul and Sienna had expertly broken down the tent—I'd stood nearby, painfully aware of just how useless I was.

Once everything was returned to our backpacks, all we had to do was wait. We sat around the firepit watching the dying embers.

"How much longer will we be here?" Paul tried to sound casual, but I knew his secret. He had his perfect proposal spot in mind.

I shook my head. It's not that I wanted to be the bearer of bad news, but Paul had to know the truth. "My guess, a minimum of two hours."

"Yeah," Paul said. "I was afraid of that." He scrubbed his face with his hands and muttered something about "...Holt had to find another dead body."

The family had also broken down their tent, but they didn't join us on the logs around the fire. In general, I prefer as little interaction with strangers as possible. Still, it was weird how standoffish they were.

Either they were actually scared we were a group of murderers, or they had something to hide.

"What kind of illegal things do people do in the woods?" I asked.

Britt's hand moved to cup my neck, a gesture that was supposed to be soothing. "I'm really sorry someone was killed while we were backpacking, but this hardly ever happens."

I frowned. "Not the murder." I spoke low to keep the other group from hearing. "I meant that family. If none of them killed the younger brother, what could they be hiding?"

"That's interesting." Paul leaned closer, apparently taking my question seriously.

"And what illegal activity would require hiking in the woods?" Sienna added, rolling a dreadlock between her fingers.

"Hunting for endangered species?" Britt suggested.

We all turned to look at their gear—realizing a moment too late how suspicious all of us looking at the same time was. Then, in unison, we all looked away...It wasn't subtle, and Hiker Dad definitely noticed.

"I don't see any hunting gear," Paul said.

"Or signs that they're carrying traps," Sienna added.

Before more suggestions could be made, the dad came over, his shoulders puffed out. "Can I help you?"

Why was he so jumpy?

If my baby sister Juniper were here, she'd be able to spout out a convincing lie. As it was, the four of us froze. I finally said, "Paul was telling us your backpacks are the trending brand right now."

The guy's cold eyes stared at me, clearly waiting for more.

"Uhh...do you think the quality is worth the extra money?"

"I don't know yet," Hiker Dad grumbled before wandering back to the other side of the campsite.

I let out a sigh as Sienna whispered, "He's definitely hiding something."

"But what?" Britt asked. "All four of them are acting strange. But I doubt they committed a group murder."

"Well"—Paul's eyes gleamed in the mischievous way Britt's did—"maybe one of them killed the backpacker and the other three found out. They're all keeping it secret."

"I've heard dumber ideas," I muttered—before realizing I wasn't caffeinated enough to keep myself from verbalizing inappropriate comments.

Paul laughed. "See, our detective agrees. Think about it. If Brittany told us she'd killed that man, we'd do what we could to help her get away with it."

I opened my mouth to disagree, but hesitated. There'd been a moment on our first date when I was sure Britt had killed five people, and I'd been fine with it. If she ever committed murder, I'd trust she had her reasons.

"Is that what happened?" Sienna asked. "One of them is the killer, and the rest are covering it up?"

"Probably not," Paul said. "But it's a theory."

"My money's on the missing hikers," I said.

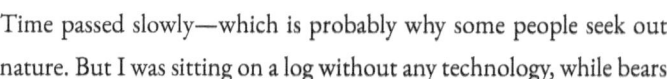

Time passed slowly—which is probably why some people seek out nature. But I was sitting on a log without any technology, while bears and murderers prowled the woods.

Maybe an hour later, the whirring of the helicopter returned. This time it didn't hover at the campsite but a little ways off, likely right where the body was.

The chopper stayed there for so long, I was at risk of long-term hearing damage. Finally, Britt pointed to where a large neon basket could be seen through the trees as it rose up and into the chopper. A minute later, the helicopter began its journey back to civilization. Shortly after, Cop Kid and Ranger Trees returned.

They came straight to where we sat. When Ranger Trees looked at us, there was a new glimmer of interest. "Since apparently you all have experience with police interviews, I'll start with the other group."

"Of course," Britt said—while Paul reached reflexively to the pocket that held the engagement ring.

"No rush," Paul agreed, somehow sounding relaxed.

I was a little too tired and way undercaffeinated to worry about staring as Ranger Trees led each member of the family away for a private interview in the forest.

The young man and his girlfriend both seemed relatively calm. Yet for how anxious Hiker Dad and Uptight Daughter were acting, you'd think they were hiding a skull in one of their backpacks...Actually, was there a skull hidden in their backpacks?

Hiker Dad gave his daughter a meaningful glance as the ranger led him away.

"Could their family have found something valuable?" I asked.

"What, like buried gold?" Paul's suggestion was pure sarcasm.

I rolled my eyes. "Yes. My theory is they found pirate treasure."

Britt's mouth twitched as she fought her smile. "I don't know. Pirate treasure would be pretty heavy. How much gold could two people really carry in their backpacks?"

"Fair point," I said. "What weighs less than pirate treasure?"

"Feathers!" Sienna said, seeming unusually excited.

I frowned. While we'd all been joking about treasure, Sienna appeared serious about her feather suggestion.

"Uh-huh. Feathers are lighter than gold." It was impossible to hide the skepticism from my voice. No way the hikers were hiding contraband feathers.

Or that's what I thought until Britt said, "Sienna, you might be right about the feathers."

My frown deepened. Britt *wasn't* kidding. What was I missing?

Paul nodded—apparently he was also on board.

"What's going on?" I asked.

For a moment they all stared at me like they thought I was kidding.

"Oh, uh..." Britt tucked an invisible strand of hair behind her ear. "Certain birds, like bald eagles, are extremely protected. Owning a single feather comes with a serious fine and possible jail time."

"Then why—" I'd started to ask why anyone would have an eagle feather, but I figured out the answer. Because they were protected, certain people wanted them.

I chose a different question. "How much is a bald eagle feather worth?"

Paul squinted up at the sky. "While I don't know the details, I'm guessing they're worth enough money that opportunists might collect them if they happened upon a dead bird. But I doubt they're worth enough for people to go out hunting."

"Gotcha," I said.

It wasn't a great motive, but maybe Younger Brother had seen them steal feathers off a dead eagle. If he threatened to go to the police, maybe Uptight Daughter snapped and killed him instead.

My attention was caught by Hiker Dad's return. Uptight Daughter was the last person in their group to be interviewed. I caught the slightest shake of the head from Hiker Dad as they passed each other.

Maybe it was eagle feathers. Maybe it was murder. Whatever the case, those two were hiding something.

Chapter 7

I watched as Hiker Dad sat by his son and his son's girlfriend. They shared no secretive stares or guilty glances. Whatever Hiker Dad was hiding, his son didn't know about it.

Once Uptight Daughter returned, Ranger Trees came to our group. "Holt Jacobs, we might as well get this over with."

Get *what* over with?

As if realizing his poor choice of words, Ranger Trees cleared his throat. "What I meant to say is, Holt, if you would follow me, I'll take your statement."

"Sure thing," I said. As I left, my eyes momentarily locked with Sienna's. Her peaceful, mother-earth vibe had changed into surprise from the ranger's comment. I raised an eyebrow, as if to say, *What can you do?*

Once we were a little ways down a footpath, the ranger gestured to a rock. Apparently, that was my seat for the interview. Before he could ask a question, his radio crackled. "We're almost there. Vincent is running out of energy. It's been slow going."

"Copy that," Ranger Trees said. Once the radio went silent, he asked, "What time was it when people moved past your tent?"

I blinked. Who was Vincent?

Could it be Older Brother or Broke Friend? If so, would the person be able to tell us what happened last night?

"Holt." The ranger's voice was stern.

"Yeah?"

"We've got this. We're using all our resources to make sure Kyle gets justice. All you have to do is answer my questions, then go back to enjoying your vacation."

I raised an eyebrow. If Cop Kid were there, he'd be covering a laugh with a cough.

I couldn't ignore murder.

It was also impossible for me to enjoy nature.

Do you know what nature is? Mosquitoes...and other bugs that dive straight for your ears.

None of our interviews took long. Once the final one was complete, we waited as the police strode around looking official.

The delay must've gotten to Hiker Dad because at one point he stood and approached the ranger, who was talking quietly with Cop Kid. "When can we leave?"

"Soon." Ranger Trees's dark eyes stared at Hiker Dad as he sized the man up. "We have your statements and contact information. I'm expecting colleagues on the trail. They're bringing a witness. You'll need to sit tight until they get here."

Hiker Dad grumbled about getting lost in the dark if they didn't leave soon. But he returned to his family, and they began eating a lunch of granola bars. Britt must've taken that as a sign we should also start eating because suddenly a variety of granola bars were making the rounds.

I shouldn't complain, but not only was I without real coffee, running water, or technology, but my lunches for the trip would be granola bars...a food that was barely edible on a good day.

Paul had just brewed a new pot of instant coffee when the sounds of approaching hikers broke through the white noise of nature.

At once, Ranger Trees strode toward the trail, with Cop Kid right behind him. I stood but didn't leave my spot as we all waited for the new set of rangers and the mysterious witness.

Would it be Broke Friend or Older Brother?

A woman in her midforties led the way. At first from my angle all I could see was a pair of legs behind her—not who belonged to them.

It wasn't until after Ranger Trees and Cop Kid had greeted her that she moved, revealing Broke Friend.

His skin was paleish and damp with sweat. He stumbled near the firepit before collapsing to the ground. His eyes kept blinking, which meant he hadn't passed out. Didn't matter that he was probably fine. Britt was instantly by his side.

First, she helped him move, until he was slumped against a log. Britt asked, "Do you have any health conditions I should know about?"

Broke Friend shook his head.

I was surprised Ranger Trees wasn't right beside Brittany, interrogating Broke Friend. Instead, he stood talking quietly with the female ranger. They must have been comparing notes.

"Let me get you some water," Britt said. Before she could move, a new ranger appeared carrying two backpacks—one on his back and one on his chest.

"Here's his pack and his water," the man said in a deep voice.

"What's wrong with him?" I asked.

The man shook his head. "It's exhaustion." As he set down the front pack, I thought I heard, "And he's an idiot," but I could have made that up.

Britt gave Broke Friend his water, then checked his pulse and pupils. His shirt was splotchy with sweat, and he really seemed off. Was it hot enough for heat exhaustion?

When Britt asked if he'd been injured, he shook his head.

"No injuries. I'm just tired."

Killing a man could do that. But I couldn't really ask, *Are you tired from killing your friend?*

I felt Britt's eyes on me. Had she read my mind?

"Have you been backpacking before?" Britt asked in her professionally polite paramedic voice.

Broke Friend nodded. His eyes were almost closed before they popped open again. "I've been backpacking plenty. I hiked up here yesterday, then I hiked down last night, and now"—he yawned—"I had to hike back up again."

Britt asked, "Did you get any sleep?"

"No." And Broke Friend rubbed at his eyes like that would solve a sleepless night.

"Why did you leave in the middle of the night?" I asked. "Isn't it dangerous to hike in the dark?"

"And alone," Paul added.

"You heard what happened here last night?" Broke Friend's eyes were dark.

"I've heard some," I hedged, since I wasn't sure if he was referencing the murder.

"Yeah, well"—Broke Friend struggled to sit up—"we had a big fight last night. I knew if I stayed around, there'd be trouble." He gave a sort of sick smile. "Look, I'm sorry Kyle's dead, but if I hadn't escaped down the mountain, Nick would have killed me, too."

Nick? Who is Nick?

"Nick is the one getting married?" Britt's voice kept its controlled calm—though her question was more of a detective question than a paramedic question.

"Yeah, Nick, he…" Broke Friend placed a hand over his mouth like he was battling a round of nausea. "He got really mad when we said his fiancée was wrong for him."

Beside me, Paul's eyes darted quickly to Sienna before looking away. Paul's entire body had tensed. While I doubted Paul would kill me if I said he shouldn't marry Sienna, he would be understandably upset.

"You saw Nick kill Kyle?" asked Britt.

"No," Broke Friend admitted. "But Nick was so mad. Who else could be the killer?"

It was an interesting question. What I needed was a clearer timeline of when everything happened last night. I began asking, "Do you know what time you started down the tra—"

"Excuse me," Ranger Trees's voice interrupted me. "But I would like to talk to the witness in private."

"Of course," I said.

Cop Kid was smirking, which was all the encouragement I needed. "Brittany's a paramedic. She was examining him."

"And what were *you* doing?" Ranger Trees asked.

I assumed the question was rhetorical and chose not to answer. He hadn't sounded angry, more disappointed, like he expected more from me.

Since Broke Friend was unwilling to move from his spot on the ground, we left the campfire and stood over by the tree our backpacks were resting against.

"What do you think?" I asked.

Britt shrugged. "He's not faking the exhaustion."

"But does that mean we cross him off our list of suspects?" Sienna asked.

I shook my head. "I don't know. He could have left our camp, snuck back later, killed…"

"Kyle," said Britt.

"Killed Kyle," I continued. "Then gone back down the mountain."

Paul rubbed a hand along his jaw. "He'd be exhausted either way."

"Could we test his alibi if we knew the trail he took?" Sienna asked.

"Doubtful," Paul said. "With him hiking alone in the dark, he'd be moving slower. There'd be no real way of figuring out how far he *should* have gone."

By the firepit, Ranger Trees was still speaking with Broke Friend, but now as he talked he was also unrolling the sleeping bag from Broke Friend's backpack.

I squeezed my eyes shut. I was too wound up to *want* a nap. Yet the sleeping bag caused my temples to tingle with the reminder of an almost sleepless night and a lack of quality caffeine.

"Will they let us keep hiking?" Paul's main concern clearly wasn't solving a murder. It was getting to Infinity Falls.

No one answered. Instead, we continued watching. Broke Friend stretched out on top of the sleeping bag. Ranger Trees waited until Broke Friend was asleep before joining Hagen and the two other rangers.

On the other side of the camp, the family of hikers watched with similar expressions of concern. Hiker Dad was talking as he gestured up the trail. Why did they want to keep hiking?

That didn't make sense.

If any of their group had killed Younger Brother, you'd think they'd want to get off the mountain as fast as possible. Or if they were smuggling contraband eagle feathers, that would also be a reason to leave.

Yet instead of being worried about the killer, they were concerned they couldn't keep hiking.

What possible reason could they have to stay?

"Look," Paul said. "We've got Holt's thinking face."

I raised an eyebrow. The way Paul said it, my *thinking face* sounded like I looked constipated.

Instead of replying to Paul's comment, I asked, "Why would that group want to stay on the mountain?"

"Unfinished business?" Sienna suggested.

I nodded. But what did they hope to accomplish, and how would we figure that out?

Ranger Trees turned his head to find us all staring. He waved his hand and said, "All right, come on over."

Both groups did as requested, with at least Paul holding his breath.

"We have all the information we need from you at this time," Ranger Trees said. "We'll contact you if we have any follow-up questions. You're free to hike back to your vehicles."

Uptight Daughter gasped, and Hiker Dad wrapped his arm around her. While disappointed, they were more accepting than Paul.

Paul stepped forward. "What if we don't want to go?"

Ranger Trees's attention had shifted back to the other rangers. He raised an eyebrow. "Excuse me?"

"Do we have to leave the mountain? Or are we allowed to continue hiking?"

"There's a murderer on the loose." Ranger Trees said the words slowly, like Paul might have forgotten. "You want to *keep* hiking?"

"Yes," Paul answered almost before Ranger Trees finished asking the question.

Hiker Dad raised his hand. "We would also like to keep going."

"You realize I can't guarantee your safety," Ranger Trees's dark eyes focused on each of us, making sure we understood.

Paul crossed his arms. "All due respect, but wouldn't the killer try to get away by going down the mountain?"

"That's a possibility," Ranger Trees admitted.

"If we walked back down the trail, we could run into the killer," Paul pointed out. "It'd be much safer for us to continue up the mountain."

Ranger Trees glanced at his cousin.

Cop Kid shrugged. "I said they were trouble."

"I don't recommend staying," Ranger Trees said in his most official voice.

A vein in Paul's temple pulsed. "Are you closing the mountain?"

Ranger Trees shook his head like he was disappointed in all of us. "No. The mountain isn't officially closed."

A cheer erupted. I'm not sure who all joined in. Personally, I was too busy trying to keep my lunch down to shout with joy.

Paul couldn't hide his smile, and everyone in the other group relaxed. Don't get me wrong. I was happy for Paul. But the ranger's announcement meant we wouldn't be returning to civilization anytime soon.

"Hold up." Ranger Trees raised an authoritative hand. "If you proceed, be careful, and let us know what trails you'll be on."

"Remember, the state rangers are officially discouraging you from continuing your hikes," Cop Kid said calmly. "And keep an eye out for murderers."

Ranger Trees shot his cousin an annoyed look but didn't comment.

Paul and Hiker Dad began explaining their routes to the rangers. As they talked, I wandered over to the tent the bachelor party had stayed in.

"Look but don't touch," Cop Kid said in his easygoing way.

I raised an eyebrow. "Do you think I make a habit of contaminating crime scenes?"

Cop Kid's eyes crinkled. "You never know."

He picked up a discarded walking stick and gently lifted the tent flap.

Britt was right. The tent's interior was utter chaos. Not only were both sleeping bags a mess, but shoes were strewn randomly around the space.

Hold on.

Shoes?

I began counting. There were two pairs of shoes—or four shoes total. Since this was a backpacking trip, and you had to carry all of your supplies, it was pretty safe to assume each man had traveled with only the shoes on their feet.

I checked where Broke Friend was stretched out on the sleeping bag. He wore boots.

Younger Brother's body only had socks, which meant one pair of shoes belonged to him.

There was a final pair of shoes. They must belong to Older Brother. But he was missing.

Why had he left camp without shoes?

CHAPTER 8

"**A**re they looking for him?" I asked.

"Who?" Cop Kid eased the tent flap back down.

"The murdered guy's brother. The one who's getting married. Are people searching for him?"

Cop Kid's normally relaxed face tightened. "We're doing our best. Right now a lot of rangers are working to rescue a group of college students after a rockslide."

Rockslide? Add that to the list of things to be worried about in nature.

"Why?" Cop Kid asked. "Do you think Nick killed his brother?"

"Maybe." I shrugged. "What I know is he ran off without shoes."

Instead of asking why I thought Nick was shoeless, Hagen relifted the tent flap and peered inside. After counting shoes, he gave a quick nod. "Yes. It's unlikely Nick is wearing shoes."

I nodded. The question was, did that make Nick a better or worse suspect?

If in the heat of the moment, Older Brother had killed Younger Brother, he may have been paranoid, thinking everyone was chasing him, and run off without shoes. But what if someone else killed Younger Brother, and Nick ran off because he feared for his life? Either option explained why he'd leave without proper footwear.

It didn't clear up whether or not he was the murderer.

Broke Friend snorted in his sleep loud enough that it caught our attention.

"What'll happen to him?" I asked.

Cop Kid shrugged. "Thorne took his statement. At this point there's not much more we can do. Our priority needs to be finding Nick. We need to make sure he doesn't die from the elements and ask what happened."

I scanned the trees. It was scary enough being out in the wilderness. I couldn't imagine running into the night without shoes or my backpack.

Broke Friend twitched in his sleep and rolled over.

"Isn't he a suspect?" I asked.

Cop Kid grinned. "Technically, you're all suspects. Should we sit everyone down around the campfire and wait until one of you confesses?"

I rolled my eyes. "No, thanks."

The crunch of footsteps alerted us to Britt's approach. "Are you ready?" Her pack was already secured to her back.

I looked over at Cop Kid, who nodded. "Keep an eye out for bare footprints."

"He could be wearing socks," I countered.

"Copy that." Cop Kid's eyes crinkled, and he held out his hand. "Good seeing you again."

We shook. "Same," I agreed.

Britt waited until we'd rejoined the other two to ask, "Who's wearing socks?"

"Oh, we think the older brother might not have his shoes."

"That's weird," Sienna said—which really meant something since I'm betting Sienna walked around barefoot more often than was good for her.

"That's what we thought." I hoisted on my backpack. "How far are we going today?"

"We were supposed to get to Infinity Falls tonight and spend all day there tomorrow, but with the delays, we'll see if everyone can walk fast enough to make it while there's daylight." Paul didn't quite look me over from head to toe, but a muscle in his cheek twitched.

Apparently, I was the weakest link. That was what I got for preferring treadmills over trails. Whatever. Paul's opinion didn't matter. I was here for Britt.

I clipped the straps across my chest and took one last look at our camp. The rangers had begun examining the abandoned bachelor party tent. The hiker family was also preparing to depart, and Broke Friend lay sleeping by the firepit, apparently dead to the world.

In the moment I'd spent examining the campsite, Paul had started hiking at a brisk pace. He could no longer hide his impatience—he had a romantic waterfall to get to.

I tried to match Paul's pace, with Brittany and Sienna following behind. I did all right for a while, but the elevation change started kicking my butt and I began panting. I unclipped the backpack strap across my chest to keep my lungs from being too constricted. Still, with Paul's perfect proposal on the line, I tried not to slow down.

I stumbled against a rock that stuck out of the dirt in the trail. When I tripped a second time, Britt called, "Pause."

Paul stopped. "What's wrong?"

"Time for a break," Britt said.

Paul's eyes flicked to me. "Right."

I would have been embarrassed, but I was too busy slicking back my sweaty, poofy hair.

There was a fallen tree I half sat on. My breathing was off, and it seemed like Britt was battling between going full paramedic while trying not to be an overprotective girlfriend.

"What's the rush?" Britt asked.

Paul shrugged, not quite pulling off casual. "We're supposed to make it to Infinity Falls tonight."

Britt waited, probably expecting more of an explanation, but when Paul stayed silent, she nodded. "I see." Britt was trying not to be overly worried about my health—not that I minded the attention. It was funny seeing Brittany attempting to hide the concerned glances she sent in my direction.

Sienna, however, wasn't shy. She came and perched on the tree next to me, her legs dangling off the ground due to our height difference. She reached behind me and retrieved one of my water bottles. "You must be thirsty."

I grabbed the bottle, and once my breathing had regulated, I took a long drink.

While I tried to hide it, having the whole group wait for me was embarrassing. Paul was impatient. Britt was trying not to be overprotective. And Sienna was closely monitoring my water intake.

I wasn't exactly ready to continue hiking, but I couldn't stand the awkwardness any longer. After one final drink, I stood. "We ready?"

Paul's only answer was to start hiking. Britt said quietly, "I'll keep an eye on him," before following her brother. Sienna held out her hand, and I helped her down. She had an exasperated smile. "One thing I love about the Asatos is their intense focus. But sometimes..."

"They're overfocused?" I finished.

Sienna nodded. "You can't talk to them when they're like this."

"That's what I figured."

I tried to keep an eye out in case Paul's trail was the one Older Brother had used for an escape route. It was easy to do, since there were enough roots and rocks sticking out of the path that most of my focus was already on the ground in front of me. But I had yet to spot any imprints of bare feet in the dirt.

As the day wore on, mine and Sienna's paces slowed. While she was a more experienced backpacker, the speed Paul and Britt were walking wasn't doable for their dates.

Sometimes the siblings would disappear from view for minutes at a time. Then they'd be waiting around a bend. Yet as soon as we appeared, they took off again.

I'm not an expert in the romance department, but Paul was planning on proposing. Ditching his girlfriend didn't seem like the right move. I would have mentioned this, but he was always too far away.

Couldn't Britt make him slow down?

"You know, don't you?" Sienna asked.

Had she read my mind? Had I done something to give away Paul's secret? I tried to play dumb. "Huh?"

"Paul's going to propose at Infinity Falls." Sienna's smile was radiant.

"What?" My eyes got big, and I put a hand to my heart, like I'd received shocking news...Sienna saw through my act.

"He wants it to be a surprise," Sienna said. "But it was easy to figure out."

"Yeah, Paul hasn't been subtle," I agreed. "Choosing a location named Infinity Falls has enough symbolism to imply a proposal plan."

"I'd be surprised if Paul had planned a trip to the Caves of Doom," Sienna commented.

I laughed. "That has all kinds of bad symbolism...I wonder why the bachelor party didn't choose that destination." It'd been a joke, yet we both sobered at the reference.

"It's too pretty out here to commit murder," Sienna said.

I gave a noncommittal nod. While I don't get what the big deal about a few pine trees is, I also hadn't felt the urge to murder anyone.

Britt says nature is peaceful, but the emotion I was feeling wasn't peace. If anything, I felt anxious.

In the stillness, Sienna's question from the boulder came to mind. *How were things between Britt and me?* I thought they were good. Did Sienna know something I didn't?

I was startled when Sienna asked, "Do you have a headache?"

"Uh...not really." It wasn't a total lie. Technically, I had a headache. That was to be expected. I'd barely slept and hadn't had a good cup of coffee in over twenty-four hours. But it wasn't a *bad* headache.

Apparently, my answer wasn't good enough for Sienna.

She placed a hand on my arm, and we stopped walking. "What's bothering you?"

I shifted from one foot to the other. This was inconvenient. Sienna could tell if I was lying, but I didn't want to admit the truth.

Finally, I answered. "I was wondering why you asked how things were with me and Britt."

When Sienna didn't immediately speak, I replayed my words. Had I said something wrong? Had it sounded like I was flirting?

Sienna surprised me by reaching up and tapping my nose. "Don't overthink it."

My eyebrows rose.

"Fine." Sienna held up her hands. "I'm being nosy. With Paul proposing, I was wondering if...uh, if being around Britt makes you the happiest you've ever been."

I stared at her.

"Yes, I'm happy," I said.

"Good" was Sienna's reply.

We resumed walking.

I replayed Sienna's words: *the happiest you've ever been*. Why had she asked that? Was I missing something?

An exposed root caused me to stumble. This wasn't working. With the hiking, the dead body, and the runaway man, I didn't have the energy to dig deeper into another mystery.

Sienna and I walked out of a highly wooded area to a section of mountain that was nothing but rocks and boulders. With how the trail curved, we'd be going up multiple switchbacks. That section would take a while.

"Hold on." I'd been battling the urge to have some privacy between the trees. I'd put it off because it was an awkward thing to mention to my girlfriend's brother's girlfriend. But I didn't want to wait for the next time we had tree cover.

I set my pack down, and Sienna followed suit. We left the trail in separate directions for necessary privacy. When we returned to the trail, Brittany and Paul had turned around on the rocky slope and were walking toward us.

"What's wrong?" Paul called.

"Bathroom," I shouted back.

Britt and Paul started talking to each other, but they were too far away to hear.

Once our packs were back on, we started walking on the rocky trail. Britt and Paul stood waiting. At any moment I expected them to turn around and resume walking.

Somewhere overhead there was a strange, almost rustling noise. I stopped and peered up the slope, trying to see. For where the sun was, the light was blinding.

The sound happened again.

"What is that?" I asked Sienna.

"Hm?" Sienna looked at me expectantly, waiting for the sound to repeat.

The noise shifted to the light clattering of a pebble bouncing down the slope. The sound grew louder. I shielded my eyes from the sun. Far up the hillside, I barely saw a barefoot man climbing over a boulder.

"Hey!" I shouted, but my voice was swallowed in the clatter of rocks crashing down the slope.

Hold on.

Was this a rockslide?

The instant the thought occurred, I started to run toward Britt. But Sienna caught my arm. I was stronger and could have wrestled away, but it gave the logical side of my brain the chance to realize that Britt was too far away. Breaking my neck trying to get to her wouldn't help anyone.

Sienna tugged at my arm, and we jogged back to the safety of the tree line. We found wider trees and stood behind them in case a stray boulder rolled past.

"Did you see them?" I asked a little breathlessly.

Sienna shook her head. A couple of her dreadlocks had fallen from her bun, and she was the most frazzled I'd ever seen.

"They...Paul...or Paul and Britt, they were close to where the rocks were falling."

I stared at where the trail had been, trying to catch a glimpse of either Asato, but the only view was of clouds of dirt with rocks whizzing past. I squeezed my eyes shut as my heart began to pound.

Brittany *had* to be all right.

An eternity later, the crash of stones began to quiet.

"Brittany!" I bellowed as loudly as I could right as Sienna called, "Paul!"

We both fell silent, hoping for an answering call.

Nothing.

Stray rocks were still tumbling down the slope. The whole hillside would be extremely treacherous, but I didn't care. I had to find Britt.

I left the tree cover and approached the mounds of stones that covered the trail.

"Britt!"

A second later Sienna shouted, "Paul!"

Before I had a chance to listen for an answer, I had a severe sneezing attack. The air was gritty with dirt. Every inhale triggered another sneeze.

My sneezing got so bad, I doubled over and nearly fell with the weight of my backpack. Sienna got close and tried to hand over a water bottle. She took a step back when I almost headbutted her with an extra-violent sneeze.

Through the sneezing, a faint and echoey sound reached my ears. It sounded like "Holt."

My head snapped up. Was that Britt?

I tried to call back but sneezed partway through. My answer was something like, "Briii-choo!"

"Paul?" Sienna yelled, accidentally sloshing water on my shoe.

"Yeah" came Paul's distant reply.

My eyes were watering so bad with all the sneezes that I could barely see, yet I knew the instant Sienna left my side to scramble up the rocks that separated us from the Asatos.

I pulled my T-shirt over my nose in an attempt to stop inhaling dust, but I was still sneezing when I followed Sienna.

My eyes were bleary, and I nearly broke an ankle as a rock I'd been standing on shifted. But I was too relieved that Britt was alive to notice.

A midsize boulder whizzed between Sienna and me. Someone shrieked. It sounded like Brittany.

When Paul met us, his eyes were dark. It was a level of upset I'd seen mirrored in Britt's face when we were at the winery.

He waited until after he'd lifted Sienna back onto the trail that remained and brought us far enough away from stray boulders before asking, "Are you crazy? You shouldn't have done that. Do you know how dangerous that was?"

"I had to see you." Sienna cupped Paul's face in her hand.

"You could have been killed," Paul murmured—or, I'm pretty sure that's what he said. He was talking with his face smashed into Sienna's dreadlocks and was holding her like he'd never let go.

Ordinarily, I'd be a self-conscious third wheel to such an intimate moment, but I had a different Asato I needed to wrap in my arms and never let go.

The problem was Paul and Sienna were blocking my way. Britt was standing just behind them, her face tight.

I *needed* to hold her. I pulled my shirt down from around my mouth and was about to say, *Excuse me*, to get the couple to move out of my way, but I sneezed instead. Paul moved, still clinging tightly to Sienna. I sneezed two more times as I carefully walked around them.

"Britt," I breathed, and without really thinking about it, I hoisted her into the air.

"Holt—" Her voice held a note of pain.

I immediately set her down. "What's wrong?" I scanned her body for injuries. "Were you hurt? Is it your ankle?"

Since I was facing her, I almost missed the streaks of red along the back of her arm. I moved to examine the area. There were lots of cuts and scratches, starting at her right elbow and disappearing into her T-shirt. Based on the grime along the right side of her shirt and backpack, there were more cuts hidden by her shirt.

"Britt?" My voice held an unusual amount of emotion. Instantly, I began easing her backpack off her shoulders. Instead of her blank paramedic mask, Britt made a sound that was almost a laugh, and her eyes were vacant.

"Where's your first aid kit?" I asked, realizing I needed to be the levelheaded one.

First aid kit snapped Britt out of her daze. "Why? Were you injured?"

I shook my head and crouched by her pack. "You're the one who's bleeding."

Britt craned her neck to look at her arm, then shook her head. "It's only a few scratches."

I began unzipping pockets, looking for the kit Britt always carried.

Britt sat heavily in the dirt beside where I was crouching. When she spoke, her voice was strangely hollow. "I should check you for signs of shock."

I raised an eyebrow.

I wasn't the one in shock.

Chapter 9

B ritt raised a shaky hand to cup the scruff along my jaw. I think she meant to check my pupils, but the way her eyes darted back and forth, she wasn't able to focus long enough to complete the task.

I moved my head away from her hand and kissed her fingers as I broke the contact. "Let me get you patched up. After that, you can check for signs of shock."

Britt gave a delayed nod. She was staring at the rocks that ruined our trails. Her eyes were watering, but that could have been from the dust.

I finally found the first aid kit and could start cleaning up Britt's arm. I stared at the supplies. In a general sense I knew what to do. Still, I checked to see if Paul or Sienna was available to help. They were standing in an embrace, whispering romantic things to each other. I'd be doing this by myself.

Tucked away in the red bag was a small pocketknife—maybe a pen knife? At any rate, it looked like something you'd give a child.

I put on a pair of disposable gloves. Her lower arm would need to be cleaned and bandaged. I gently raised the sleeve of Britt's T-shirt to check her upper arm. The fabric had done a decent job of protecting her skin. Still, I'd want to clean and disinfect the area.

If Britt were in better shape, I'd joke about this being payback for the time she cut me out of my clothes—at least I wasn't going to shave her head.

I sat in the dirt at a good angle to work on Britt's side. I opened the pocketknife. The glint of the blade caught her attention. Her posture straightened, and she almost sounded normal. "No."

"Would you relax?" I managed to grin. "I'm turning your shirt into a bro-tank."

Britt twisted to face me. "But I don't want a *bro-tank*."

I took a deep breath. I could do this. I needed to remain calm while dealing with an argumentative patient. Britt has taken care of me plenty in the time we've been together. Still, I'd like to think I'm a better patient.

"Come on," I said. "Let me help you."

For a moment Britt's eyes really focused on mine. "You'll disinfect?"

"Yes, ma'am."

"All right." She sighed. "Make me a bro-tank."

While being small, the blade was impressively sharp, and it easily cut off the sleeve and the area surrounding her armpit. Next, I grabbed both of my water bottles and handed one to Britt. "You should stay hydrated."

Britt took the bottle but didn't unscrew the cap. I took the bottle back and removed the lid. This time when Britt got the bottle, she took a few sips.

I poured water from the second bottle onto a clean cloth. Brittany winced when I began cleaning her skin. "Sorry," I murmured.

The cuts weren't bleeding much. Most were scratches that showed red between torn skin. But there was a fair amount of dust and grit embedded in her arm. It took some time, but I finally wiped away all the foreign particles.

"This'll sting," I warned as I unscrewed the tube of disinfectant. Britt tensed at the warning but didn't make a sound as I applied the ointment to her arm.

The last step was rolling gauze around her arm and shoulder. Then my battlefield doctoring was over.

After I removed my gloves, I sat back and bowed my head in my hands. Suddenly all the worry about Brittany that I'd shoved down came to the surface. And I mean truly erupting—like I jumped to my feet and put some distance from the others before puking.

When I straightened, Britt was waiting with a water bottle. Some of her usual spark had returned. "Can I check you for shock now?"

I rolled my eyes before accepting the water and rinsing out my mouth.

We returned to where Sienna and Paul remained, totally oblivious to the world around them. Had Paul decided to propose early? Skip Infinity Falls and go with a *we just survived death* proposal?

But there was no ring on Sienna's finger. Paul must be waiting.

I sat in the dirt and leaned back against a large rock. Britt made a space for herself on the ground between my legs and rested against my chest.

I needed to ask Britt if she'd seen the barefoot man right before the rockslide, but first I had to close my eyes and take deep breaths.

An unknown level of isolation surrounded us. We were trapped on a trail that was no longer a trail. Our best option was probably climbing across the rocks and backtracking. Yet, based on Paul's reaction when he saw us, that was a pretty dangerous option.

My stomach gurgled, and Britt lurched forward. "Are you going to be sick?"

"No," I said and tugged her back against my chest. I cleared my throat. A new fear arose that my breath was atrocious after vomiting.

Also, I hadn't showered since the start of this trip. All of me smelled pretty bad.

I must've tensed, because Britt said, "Relax. We're safe."

We stayed like that for a long time, with Paul and Sienna embracing and whispering to each other and Britt resting against me.

"What happened to your arm?" I realized I hadn't asked earlier. My engineering brain went straight to *fix-it* mode.

"Oh" was all Britt said. She moved to face me and tucked an invisible strand of hair behind her ear. "The first rock whizzed right behind me and Paul. We started running." She shook her head. "It was close. But just as we cleared the danger zone, I tripped over a tree root and fell."

I bent forward and kissed the gauze on her shoulder. I'm not usually this sentimental, but Britt had almost died.

My hands tightened into fists as I looked up the ridgeline. "Did you see who did it?"

"Did it?" Britt repeated. "Holt, it was an accident."

"Not exactly," I said. "The older brother was climbing over rocks right before the slide."

"He started this?" Paul asked—finally interested in something besides Sienna.

"Yeah," I said. "What I don't know is whether he meant to start the rockslide or whether it was accidental."

"Where did you see him?" Paul asked.

The view of the hillside had changed drastically. Not only had my location shifted, but the entire landscape was disturbed.

I tried not to groan as I stood up with my tired and sore muscles. "Umm..." I stared at the ridgeline. "Maybe there, by that outcropping."

Paul nodded, then yelled, "Hey!" like that would make Older Brother appear. It didn't work. Older Brother must be long gone. He'd probably killed his brother and was trying to escape.

"You're sure it was him?" Paul asked.

"Yes," I said. Though from a distance and with the sun, I wouldn't want to swear to that in front of a jury.

"I'll call the rangers," Paul said. "They'll want to know about your sighting and the rockslide."

We all listened to Paul's side of the phone call. Near the end he said, "Yes, I understand. We're all safe....I'm sure we can find the trail...If there's trouble, I'll call back."

I hadn't considered having a rescue party pluck us out of our predicament. If they'd offered help, Paul had declined. We were stranded.

Maybe I should have made the phone call. I wouldn't have turned down a helicopter ride.

When Paul hung up, Britt asked, "How do we get out of here?" Technically, the question was for the whole group, but really she was asking Paul.

Paul's shoulders expanded as he analyzed the ruined switchbacks above us. Next his gaze went to the mound of rocks Sienna and I had climbed over, and then his head dropped.

Sienna was instantly by his side, and once Brittany had stood up, she joined them.

"It'll be all right," Sienna said.

Paul shook his head. "Not this time. I thought we could have a good trip to Infinity Falls. But there's been a murder, a rockslide, and we're stuck on a rock face with a killer on the loose."

"What if we go back the way we came?" Sienna suggested.

Paul took a sharp intake of breath, real fear flashing through his eyes. "No. The two of you shouldn't have done that. One wrong step, and you'd get swept away in another slide."

As if to prove his point, a few rocks clattered past.

Paul resumed scanning the terrain above us. "There," he finally said. "We can take the deer trail."

It took a moment to find, but when I spotted his *deer trail*, I saw that it was a dirt runoff about the width of my shoe...and it led directly up. "Is that safe?" I couldn't help asking.

Paul's jaw tightened. "It's the best option we have. Walk slowly," Paul directed. "Be very careful where you put your feet."

"Paul?" Brittany didn't need to say anything else. The worry on her face did all the talking.

He swallowed, and his confidence slipped. "We'll be fine."

Paul led the way, followed by Sienna, then Britt, with me in the rear. Paul hadn't been kidding. He was moving very slowly, testing each step before trusting it with his weight.

As much as I believed Paul knew what he was doing, I didn't enjoy the steep incline. If my foot slipped on shale, I'd be sliding down an unfortunate distance.

Two thoughts.

One: Sienna better say yes when Paul proposed.

Two: Brittany better not expect me to go on another backpacking trip for the rest of the decade.

Who knew no running water would be the least of my problems?

We were nearing the top of the rocky ridge when I saw a dark reddish-brown smear on a rock. Was that blood? Had Older Brother used the deer trail? How much farther could he go without shoes or supplies?

Was staying out of jail worth starving to death in the mountains?

"Britt?" I asked, trying not to startle her on the treacherous trail. When Britt paused climbing, I continued. "Do you see that stain?"

Carefully, Britt turned to get a good look. "It's blood," she said.

"That's what I thought."

"Is that from a bare foot?" I asked.

"Hard to know for sure. If Nick's been walking this far without shoes, his feet must be bleeding." Britt turned back to the trail. My discovery meant we'd fallen behind.

I kept a close watch for more blood but didn't spot any in the dirt. The blood on the rock was practically a small pool. Like the guy had sat down to rest. And with all the nature poking up, there wouldn't be a clear blood trail to track where Older Brother went.

If we had a sniffer dog, maybe. But I doubt they'd be lowering a specialized canine from a helicopter anytime soon.

Even going slowly, walking directly up a steep incline was exhausting. It was a relief when we reached the ridgeline and Paul called a halt. "We'll take a few minutes to rehydrate, and then we'll find the trail."

I sat down and closed my eyes. A headache I'd been too stressed to notice was coming on full force. While a lack of sleep and allergies didn't help, my real problem was a caffeine deficiency.

"Here." Britt had crouched in front of me. "Have some caffeinated jelly beans."

"Huh?" I asked. (I'm a gifted conversationalist.)

"Caffeinated jelly beans," Britt repeated. "I told you about them when I was packing. Remember?"

"Yeah, I remember," I said, trying to massage away some of the tension from my temples. "Weren't you joking?"

"Not joking. Try one."

I raised an eyebrow. Britt sounded like a paramedic talking to a patient.

Maybe it was my face. At any rate, Britt's hand with the baggie of caffeinated jelly beans disappeared. "Sorry."

I felt bad. "No, I'm sorry." I grinned. "Now give me those before I bite your head off."

I don't recommend caffeinated jelly beans. They're almost powdery, but they had enough kick to lessen the throbbing in my temples.

"Ready?" Paul asked.

"Yup." I winced as I got back on my feet. Some of my muscles were already stiff.

Paul said, "If we head southeast, we should find the trail."

Britt and Sienna both nodded. I also nodded like I knew what direction was *southeast*. It's not that I *couldn't* figure it out, but I didn't know instinctively where Paul would lead us.

The animal trail we'd followed had brought us above the rockslide. The walk southeast was even slower going, without any sort of path to guide us.

Paul's neck glistened with sweat. He was feeling the pressure of being in charge of our safety. Once, as we headed toward a tree line, his foot slid. For a moment he was uncomfortably close to somersaulting down the mountainside.

Before any of us had time to react, Paul regained his footing. He kept walking like nothing had happened. It left me wondering, if Paul died, who would give Sienna the engagement ring?

I wasn't the best choice for that job. But better me than a stranger returning Paul's personal effects.

Time had taken on a surreal effect. If Britt ever convinced me to join her on another backpacking adventure, I'd need to remember to wear a watch. Paul had told me I'd want one, but I hadn't bothered to grab one. Now I was stuck in a space outside of time. But not knowing the time was better than continually asking, which would be embarrassing.

While I didn't know the actual time, the sun was getting noticeably lower in the sky and we were lost in the mountains.

It felt safer once we were back in the woods. Plenty of bad things could still happen in the forest, but at least we weren't in danger of another rockslide.

"Stay here," Paul directed as he set down his backpack. "I'll scout around to find the trail."

Brittany's chin shot up. Before she could argue, Paul said, "Make sure they eat something." Then he strode away.

Sienna and I shared an annoyed look. Neither of us appreciated being the Asatos' helpless dates. Not that they noticed. Paul was gone, and Britt was too focused on getting granola bars.

She'd even unwrapped the tops before handing them over—like we might get confused and eat the wrapper. When Britt gave Sienna a water bottle, Sienna asked, "What, no ice?"

I didn't give Britt a chance to decide whether she was joking. Instead, I asked, "Brittany, can you give me a shoulder massage?" I stretched melodramatically. "I'm really tight."

For a moment Britt reached for me, her brain in full paramedic fixer mode. Then she hesitated and looked from my face to Sienna's.

"We can get our own granola bars," I said quietly.

Britt tried to smile, but it didn't reach her eyes. "Of course."

I tugged at her hand. "I'm sure Paul's fine. Come on, sit down."

She sat but held her bar without eating and stared blankly into space.

I decided to try to redirect Britt's attention. "Does running off into the woods without shoes make the older brother the killer or a witness?"

Sienna gave an almost imperceptible nod of understanding before saying, "Running off without shoes makes me think Nick was being chased."

I said, "But if Nick was innocent, why wouldn't he ask us for help or find the rangers?"

We both looked at my girlfriend, but she remained silent.

"Brittany?" I asked.

"Hm?" She finally looked at me.

I repeated the question.

Britt frowned. "If Nick saw the murder happen, that sort of trauma could've wreaked havoc on his brain. And if he's been alone, without food or water all this time, he's suffering from hunger and dehydration. Nick won't be thinking rationally."

I leaned forward. "Would your guess be Nick's a witness instead of a prime suspect?"

"Uh, no. He's probably the killer." Britt rubbed a hand across her face. "Nick's getting married. Family brings up a lot of emotion. If they argued and he accidentally killed Kyle, he could have fled from camp with too much adrenaline to notice he wasn't wearing shoes."

I was about to answer when Britt jumped up. "Paul shouldn't have left. Last time we separated, we nearly lost each other in a rockslide."

"Paul knows what he's doing," Sienna said calmly.

"Maybe," Britt mumbled. She shook her head. "For how wild Paul was, when you were missing, I was sure he'd propose the moment he saw you."

"I'm glad he didn't," Sienna said. "That moment was already perfect."

There was silence as we let Sienna's words sink in...or there was silence until I asked a question. "Britt, you know about the proposal?"

"Of course I know. I'm his sister." Brittany frowned. "How do *you* know?"

I tapped my head. "Detective."

Britt must've had a sarcastic reply, but I was distracted by movement. In the distance, I caught the flicker of bright orange through the trees—like the orange of that weird family's backpacks.

I was on my feet in an instant. "Hey!" I shouted. "Over here."

Britt and Sienna also stood.

"What is it?" Sienna asked.

"Through those trees." I pointed. "There was a fancy backpack."

Brittany grabbed my arm. "We're close to the trail!"

CHAPTER 10

The orange I'd seen disappeared behind a tree.

"Stay with the bags," I said, and took off. I did my best to jog safely in the direction of where I'd spotted the backpack. "Over here," I shouted, with Britt and Sienna also yelling as loud as they could.

Suddenly the orange came back into view, followed by the bright blue of another backpack. They were still far away, but I think they heard us.

I tripped on an exposed root, but managed a somewhat controlled fall to the ground.

"Holt!" Britt almost shrieked.

I raised my hand in a thumbs-up before getting up and resuming my jog—though at a slower pace.

"Hello?" echoed a man's voice.

"Here. Uh..." Was I traveling southeast? It seemed likely. If I reversed the compass points, it would be the direction our rescuers could spot us. "We're northwest of you."

"Be careful," I heard right before I stumbled at a sudden dip in the ground. I needed to calm down. I didn't want to break my neck before I reached the trail. But I was too excited to care much about safety.

A figure, an actual flesh-and-blood human came into view. It was Hiker Son. He waved to me, then turned and said, "I see him."

The son gave me a friendly nod when I reached him and said, "You must've had an adventure."

"Yeah," I panted.

"Is everyone safe?" Hiker Dad had appeared and was taking charge.

Last I knew, Paul was still hunting for the trail, but his chances of survival were pretty good.

"Paul was searchi—" At that moment I sort of inhaled a bug and broke into a hacking coughing fit.

"Where are they?" Hiker Dad asked. He'd removed his backpack in preparation for a rescue mission.

I pointed, not quite ready to open my mouth and give bugs more opportunities to fly in. It wasn't the easiest to spot Britt and Sienna, but after moving closer to me, Hiker Dad nodded. "We'll make sure you all make it back to the trail."

I'm guessing he thought I'd stay behind while he completed a solo rescue mission, but I wanted to personally escort Britt to the trail—that way I'd show her what roots were tripping hazards. Besides, I'd left my backpack, and a man should carry his own pack.

The return trip seemed to stretch out. Occasionally, I would lose sight of Britt or Sienna, but they always came back into view.

"Why aren't they coming to meet us?" Hiker Dad asked.

At first I couldn't think of the answer, but when I remembered, I felt foolish for having forgotten. "It's Paul. He told us to stay and that he'd be back. They won't leave until they see Paul."

As we grew closer, I was just opening my mouth to yell a greeting when a man calling, "Holt!" from behind had me stumbling as I spun around.

There, a little ways down the hillside, was Paul walking toward us.

I don't know why I expected Paul to be limping—it's not like we'd been separated for very long—but it was a surprise to see that he was uninjured.

I yelled, "We found the trail. I spotted"—*what were the names of the hiker family?*—"the other hikers on the trail. How did you know to come back?"

Paul's grin was relieved as he called back, "I heard all the racket you were making. I was worried you'd met a bear."

"Or a skunk," I muttered.

"What's that?" Hiker Dad asked.

I shook my head. "Nothing."

As happy as I was to see Paul again, it didn't compare with Sienna or Britt. My girlfriend's entire face lit up, while Sienna gave a shriek so high, it caused hearing damage. Sienna came rushing down to meet Paul.

Hiker Dad resumed walking, and I followed. Soon enough I was wrapping my arms around Britt and kissing her.

"You smell nice," I murmured.

Britt laughed and broke away. "I smell like sweat."

I shrugged. "Whatever. The scent is working."

Hiker Dad hefted Paul's backpack onto his back, partially hitting me in the back.

"Umm..." I said. Had he done that on purpose? Was he trying to stop Britt and me from kissing?

He had been in a hurry to leave Paul before Sienna reached him.

I tried to catch Britt's eye to see if she'd noticed Hiker Dad's strange behavior, but she was too busy putting on her pack.

By the time my backpack was secure, Hiker Dad was picking up Sienna's pack. I said, "I got that." If someone was going to carry two packs, it wasn't going to be a member of our rescue party.

"All set?" Britt asked, after I'd put Sienna's bag on like a front pack. "Set," I said.

As we walked, I snuck glances at Hiker Dad. Was he actually bothered by displays of affection, or was I overanalyzing? This trip, Hiker Son had brought a girlfriend. Hiker Dad must be all right with a certain level of affection.

Also, he wore a wedding ring. There were two obvious answers for that. Either Hiker Dad was married and his wife didn't go backpacking. Or, Hiker Dad was a widower who still wore the ring.

A third, less likely option would be that he's divorced. But it's fairly uncommon for divorced people to keep wearing their rings.

There are plenty of other reasons someone *might* wear a wedding ring, but those bizarre options only happen in Britt's romantic comedies.

Still, if Hiker Dad was currently married, he must be uncomfortable with public displays of affection—or he never touched his wife.

If he was widowed, it was grief over the reminder of what he'd lost.

And, if divorced, he might find any sort of romance a shallow lie.

Upon closer inspection, Hiker Dad looked a little...off. Like someone who'd suffered a recent illness or had terrible insomnia. Did any of that make him a likely candidate for murder? If Hiker Dad had insomnia, he might have left the tent in the middle of the night. And if he'd caught Younger Brother doing something illegal, he might be more involved with the murder than he'd admitted.

"...take my pack now," Sienna said.

I blinked. I'd been moving on autopilot, lost in my thoughts, and hadn't noticed we'd reached Sienna and Paul.

"Sure," I finally said and removed her backpack. Since I was already holding it, I helped Sienna get her arms through the straps—ordinarily Paul's job, but I figured he wouldn't mind.

"Do you know how much farther you're going before you reach your campsite?" Paul asked Hiker Dad.

He shrugged. "Once we get back to the trail, maybe one and a half miles."

"That's good," Paul said. "It's getting late." He cast a worried glance in my direction.

Was Paul still concerned about me? I'd handled today's events remarkably well. And I'd gotten us back to the trail.

But Paul's focus wasn't on me. I twisted around. Just behind me, Britt was walking. She kept up with us, yet she was moving slowly. Her face was pale, and she tugged subconsciously at the part of her shirt I'd cut away.

I'd need to check her arm once we made it to camp—I also needed to check on her.

Hiker Son and Hiker Girlfriend stood like guideposts for us to follow. Yet Uptight Daughter only came into view once we'd actually made it onto the trail. She sat against a tree looking even sulkier than she had in the morning.

Hiker Dad nodded and said, "Amanda."

She got to her feet. "It's almost dark."

Seeing as everyone was clearly visible without the aid of flashlights, that was a serious exaggeration. But she had a point. While June is the month with the longest nights, I'm not sure how daylight works once the sun dips behind a mountain.

The shadows around us were growing longer, and we'd still need to set up camp once we got to the site.

Hiker Dad's mouth pressed together at his daughter's comment, but instead of being angry, he seemed tired...or sad.

Hiker Son let out an exasperated breath before leading the group down the path. Hiker Girlfriend followed, and pretty soon Paul and Sienna were making pleasant small talk with the couple.

I was walking in the back half with a tired father, a sullen daughter, and Britt, who no longer had the sparkle in her eyes. Usually I like quiet, but today there was a toxic feel about it.

There was obvious tension between the father and daughter. And the daughter was a little old to be in the *dad is ruining my life* phase. If she was upset with him, there had to be a reason.

I wanted to ask Britt's opinion, but I couldn't with the duo right there. Besides, Britt kept looking worse. There was an almost gray coloring to her skin.

I tried to guess how far we'd gone, but I'm not great at judging distances on dirt paths. Though I could easily tell you how many city blocks are in a mile (the answer's twenty).

Britt needed some rest. Maybe she had a concussion. I'd been too focused on her arm to consider other injuries. We should keep going while there was still daylight. It would be safest to wait until we reached camp.

Britt began rubbing her hand across the shoulder she'd fallen on.

I was an idiot.

She had to be super sore. Even with the gauze, all those scratches must be chaffing with the pressure of the backpack strap.

"Here." I paused in front of Brittany.

She blinked up at me, almost like she didn't recognize me.

"Give me your backpack."

Britt didn't even pause to consider my suggestion before saying, "No." She would have resumed walking if I weren't blocking the way.

"Come on." I rested my fingers on a shoulder strap. "Let me carry your pack."

"Why?" Britt's voice held a note of suspicion, while her face remained blank. This wasn't her paramedic mask but something worse that scared me.

I gave the backpack strap a playful tap. "Trust me, okay?"

Britt wasn't convinced.

I tried again. "I've trusted you to bring me to the hospital when I was clearly fine. Now it's your turn."

Britt sort of nodded. That was the only encouragement I needed to ease the backpack off and secure it to my chest. She raised her chin. "I am fine, by the way."

"Of course you are," I agreed.

And Britt was *almost* fine. She kept up with everyone and her shoulders relaxed, but something was off.

For my part, I was trying not to pant walking uphill with the second backpack. Even with the heat of the day cooling, I broke into a sweat. I wanted water, but I couldn't reach my bottle without help. No way was I interrupting Britt as she methodically put one foot in front of the other.

Was Britt dehydrated?

Long shadows had given way to dusk, when up ahead there came a cheer. Britt apparently didn't notice and made no reaction as we entered the clearing.

Already, Paul and Hiker Son were setting up camp on opposite sides of the clearing. Paul's and Sienna's packs were on the ground, and they were removing tent equipment. Sienna was the first to notice I carried both packs. "Your idea?"

I nodded.

Paul asked, "Has she said anything?"

I shook my head—this whole time Britt stood beside me without tracking the conversation.

"We'll get the tent up as fast as we can," Paul said. "Then she can lie down."

"Sure," I said. "I'll want to recheck her arm and go through what I remember of concussion protocol."

Britt's eyebrows twitched, the first expression I'd seen in a while. "I'm not concussed."

I froze, not sure what to say.

Paul smiled. "Good to know."

Sienna added, "Still, let's have Holt double-check."

There was a possible flicker of annoyance on Britt's face, but she said, "Okay."

Paul and Sienna got the tent set up in the time it took for me to remove Britt's sleeping bag.

Sienna crouched by the backpacks to remove soft clothes and a water bottle. She gently touched Britt's uninjured shoulder. "Do you need any tree privacy?" It was an odd expression. I assume it meant using nature's bathroom.

Britt shook her head.

"Okay," Sienna said. "Time to change." Sienna led the way into the tent, and Britt followed.

I stood frowning at the tent when Paul came to stand beside me. "Brittany's probably fine."

I raised an eyebrow.

Paul continued. "This happened a lot when we were teens right after our dad passed. Brittany can get...overloaded."

"Does she have a concussion?"

Paul lifted one shoulder. "I doubt it. Usually a good night's sleep does the trick."

"Thanks," I said.

"Uh, not to change the subject, but"—Paul was uncharacteristically embarrassed—"do you know what happened to my clean pair of underwear?"

My gaze shifted from our tent to look at Paul. "No clue."

"That's what I figured." Paul sighed. "I didn't see them in my bag when I was getting the tent equipment."

"Did you pack them?"

Paul raised his eyebrows. "I don't forget underwear."

For a five-day trip, Paul had only allowed us one extra pair of underwear. To have the pair go missing would be extremely unfortunate. Why would they go missing?

My attention shifted back to our tent. Then, realizing it was creepy to stare at the tent Britt and Sienna were changing in, I turned around to face the hiker family.

Their tent wasn't assembled. In fact, they didn't even have all the parts out.

"Have they ever camped?" I asked Paul.

"Not really," he said. "The son was a Scout, but the other three..."

Why were they here?

I wasn't a hiker. The only reason I'd strapped on my hiking boots was love. And even then, I had some regrets about agreeing to this adventure.

As we watched, Uptight Daughter removed a tarp from her pack before going to Hiker Dad's and beginning to unzip the front pocket.

"Wrong pocket!" Hiker Dad yelled, so panicked I hoped it wouldn't upset Britt.

Uptight Daughter jumped back. "You put it in the front pocket?"

Paul and I shared a look.

What were they hiding?

Chapter 11

Hiker Dad was the first to recover. "The tent poles are in the main pocket."

Uptight Daughter carefully rezipped the front pocket. Then—in a moment so fast I may have imagined it—she gave the front pocket an almost loving pat. Afterward, she got the tent poles, and the family resumed setting up like nothing weird or suspicious had happened.

I stared at the backpack's front pocket. It was approximately the size of one hiking shoe. What could be inside?

In my past crime-fighting attempts, my sister Juniper has been around. She wouldn't have felt guilty about creating a distraction and checking the pocket while no one was looking. Or she'd outright ask Hiker Dad what was inside.

There's no way I was going to ask. For starters, I don't like speaking with strangers, and even if I asked, I didn't have Juniper's skill at brainwashing people into giving me any information I wanted.

As for checking the pocket when no one was looking? The opportunity would be easy enough. All I'd have to do was wait for the family to go to bed. But that was a serious violation of privacy.

What if I found eagle feathers inside? Would I turn them in to the cops?

"She's ready," Sienna said, bending to rezip the tent to give flies the smallest window of opportunity to invade our tent.

I'd forgotten Britt's first aid kit. As I was retrieving it, Paul told Sienna, "Once we have the fire started, I'll get water boiling for supper."

"What's supper?" I asked, though I knew the answer would be, *Something freeze-dried*.

Paul shrugged. "I was thinking freeze-dried chicken curry."

"Yum," I said before grabbing Britt a granola bar. Hopefully the chicken option was less gross than last night's freeze-dried spaghetti, but Britt didn't need to stay awake to find out.

I was about to enter the tent, when Paul said, "Wait. Let's set up all the sleeping bags now."

He had a point. I grabbed the sleeping bags before returning to the tent. As soon as I crawled inside, Britt said, "I don't have a concussion."

"Right." I began unrolling the sleeping bags, careful not to knock over the lantern flashlight that lit up the tent. "I totally believe you."

Britt's eyes tightened, but she didn't reply immediately. When she spoke, it was to rattle off a series of numbers. I lost track of some of them, but it included today's date, her birthday, my birthday, when her parents were born, and when her dad died.

When she paused for air, I asked, "But what's your Social Security number?"

"Five-two-four—"

"Stop! You can't tell me that."

"Why?" Britt's face held a challenge. "It's not like you'll remember it."

"Whatever," I grumbled, having unrolled the last sleeping bag. "At least let me look at your eyes."

I sat beside her. Britt had changed into a tank top and had a light sweatshirt on her lap. While she let me check her eyes, we both knew I wasn't sure what I was looking for.

"Will you relax?" Britt asked. "I didn't hit my head when I fell. I don't have a brain bleed. Everything's fine."

I took a deep breath. Britt was in an argumentative mood, and I didn't have the energy to comment on which one of us had been in shock multiple times today. Instead, I handed her the granola bar, made sure she had water, and began unwrapping the gauze on her arm.

There were splotches of red on the bandage and parts of her shoulder were inflamed but it was nothing to be worried about. Britt flinched when I applied more antibacterial goo, but otherwise didn't comment.

"Why don't you go to bed early?" I suggested once I'd rewrapped her shoulder.

Britt had just gotten her sweatshirt over her head. She opened her mouth to disagree, then shrugged. "Okay," she agreed.

I almost asked, *Just like that?* but didn't want to push my luck.

Maybe it was overly clingy, but I couldn't leave until she was settled in the sleeping bag. I even zipped it up, like I was tucking her in for the night. Finally, I pressed a kiss on her forehead. "I love you," I murmured.

Britt probably said it back, but her voice was too soft to hear.

Quietly, I clicked off the lantern and moved to the tent's entrance, but once I touched the zipper, Britt raised her head. "Holt!" Her voice was urgent, and I was instantly by her side.

"Yeah?"

"I haven't brushed my teeth."

My chest tightened. Almost a year ago, at the winery, I'd said those words to Brittany. I knew what they meant. She wanted me to stay with her until she fell asleep. "Skip the toothbrush," I said.

Britt rolled onto her side to face me. "Really? Studies show good hygiene is one of the things people look for in a partner."

I knew what my line was. I remembered what Brittany had said months ago, yet I hated saying the words out loud. "If I break up with you tomorrow, you'll know why."

In the dimness, I caught Britt's smile.

Silence followed. It stretched on long enough that I assumed Britt was asleep. When she said, "I'm sorry," the words were quiet enough, I thought I misheard.

"Hm?"

"I'm sorry," Britt repeated. "I forced you on this trip, and it's been nothing but dead bodies and disasters."

"Hey." I found Britt's hand and laced my fingers between hers. "You didn't *force* me. Remember? *If you'll be there, I'll be there.*"

Britt sighed, and her hand relaxed.

"Does this mean you'll go on another backpacking trip?" she murmured.

I stiffened and decided to ignore her question. Britt was almost asleep, and we shouldn't start a debate about *future* backpacking trips.

Wasn't once enough?

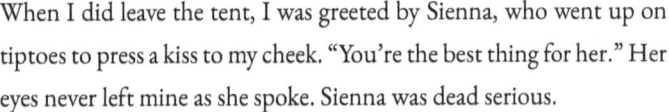

When I did leave the tent, I was greeted by Sienna, who went up on tiptoes to press a kiss to my cheek. "You're the best thing for her." Her eyes never left mine as she spoke. Sienna was dead serious.

I took a step back and managed a smooth reply that went something like, "Umm...uh..."

Paul took pity on me. "The curry's almost ready."

I nodded. I was hungry, yet the thought of eating another freeze-dried meal made my stomach flip.

I'd eat it. Partly because it was hot food, but also because the only alternative was another granola bar.

The curry was surprisingly good. I wouldn't choose the freeze-dried option in Seattle, but if I were ever stranded on the side of a mountain, the chicken curry would be a welcome addition.

We were mostly finished with dinner and Paul had just put another log on the fire, when I asked, "Do you know where we are?"

A fresh flame shot up, illuminating Paul's quick glance at Sienna.

"Yeah, we figured it out when we were walking with the Caffreys. Turns out they're also going to Infinity Falls. They were taking the beginner route. It's longer but has smoother terrain."

Wait a second. How difficult was the trail Paul tried to take us on?

Paul must've read my mind. He added, "Relax. The trail we were on was *intermediate* in difficulty. And"—another stolen glance at Sienna—"I was in a hurry."

Originally, we were supposed to reach the waterfall tonight and spend all of tomorrow hanging out.

"How far is it?"

Paul shrugged. "I don't know the exact distance. I'm hoping to get there by lunch."

We fell silent. I'm not sure if it was the sound of feet on the trail or the faint glow of headlamps flitting between the trees, but I was suddenly on my feet. "Someone's coming." Paul and Sienna also stood, and across from us, the hiker family was likewise watching the trail.

Before we could guess who the intruders were, Hagen the Cop Kid and Ranger Trees appeared.

Ranger Trees seemed momentarily concerned at the attention, a glimpse of alarm flashing through his dark eyes. But he half grunted a greeting before striding off to an unclaimed tent site.

Cop Kid, though, gave the hiker family a friendly smile and said, "Evening," before making his way to the fire. Paul gestured toward the stump he'd been sitting on—by far the best seating option—and once Cop Kid had removed his backpack, he sat down with a heavy sigh.

"Is there hot water?" Cop Kid asked as he rested his head in his hands.

Sienna said, "No, but we'll have some soon." In an instant, she'd taken the pot and marched into the darkness toward the stream.

For half a second Paul didn't move. Then his eyes widened as he remembered there was a murderer lurking around. The next instant he was jogging after her.

I raised an eyebrow. "You know how to make an entrance."

Hagen was mid-yawn, his eyes watering with the effort. When he could speak, all he did was mutter, "Some vacation."

Having removed the tent equipment from his bag, the ranger walked over and took Cop Kid's pack without so much as a glance in our direction. Cop Kid was obviously worn out, while his cousin was the opposite. Ranger Trees's body was tense, like a wild animal waiting to pounce.

Cop Kid squinted after him and mumbled something about, "...should help."

I looked from where Cop Kid was slumped with his eyes barely open to where the ranger was expertly setting up the tent. "Allow me," I offered.

Cop Kid grunted his thanks.

The ranger looked up as I approached. "Need a hand?" I offered.

The right side of Ranger Trees's mouth twitched. It was a horrible moment when I knew he knew I was a city boy who'd watch a YouTube tutorial on tent building if there was a Wi-Fi signal.

Before I could come up with an excuse that would get us both off the hook, Ranger Trees said, "Thanks. You can put together the tent poles."

I nodded and actually helped build my first tent—the one I started with Paul doesn't count. It's not like we chatted. But the ranger was patient and gave clear directions. In the end, I doubt I slowed him down too much.

I handed him their sleeping bags, and he got the interior set up. I waited as he got their water bottles and two freeze-dried bags of spaghetti from where his pack rested against a tree.

I couldn't help it. I wrinkled my nose. "Have you tried the spaghetti?"

Ranger Trees stared at me for a moment, then said, "It's better than the meat loaf," and we returned to the fire.

Paul and Sienna were back and the pot was hanging over the fire, but the water wasn't close to boiling. Cop Kid had given up any attempt to stay awake and was snoring softly, his body slumped in such a way that it seemed a gentle breeze would topple him off the stump.

"You've worn out your cousin," Paul said as a greeting.

That earned a genuine smile from Ranger Trees that was gone the next instant. All he said was, "Hagen needs to hike more."

Even with the snoring, I half expected Cop Kid to comment, but he was too far gone to care.

Ranger Trees set a water bottle on the stump beside Hagen. If I could judge his expression from the firelight, I'd say he was annoyed Cop Kid had fallen asleep by the fire. It meant the ranger was obligated to stay nearby, yet it left him alone with a group of strangers.

"Sit down," Sienna said. "You must be exhausted."

Ranger Trees nodded. "Thanks." He found a spot on the ground slightly leaning against Hagen's stump and let out a slow breath. He wasn't relaxed. If anything, he was more on edge since joining our fire.

"What can you tell us about the investigation?" Paul asked. Apparently, he cared more about the case than reading social cues.

Ranger Trees's gaze flicked to the pot like the water might magically start boiling and he'd have an excuse not to answer. But the water wasn't boiling, and the three of us were waiting while Cop Kid continued snoring.

When Ranger Trees answered, his low voice was almost melodic as he stared into the fire. "Nick Larkin is still missing and a person of interest in his brother's death. From Paul's report, everyone's trying to predict Nick's location based on a variety of factors. Hagen and I are searching the area surrounding Infinity Falls, while the rangers you saw earlier are searching farther west." The ranger shook his head. "But Nick isn't following the trails. Without much experience in the area, it's unlikely he'll survive for long, unless we find him."

"Nick's choices are dying in the woods or going to prison?" Sienna asked.

Ranger Trees nodded. "Probably."

I felt the need to add, "Unless he knows who the killer is and is trying to hide from the murderer."

"Unless that," Ranger Trees agreed, but I doubt he'd taken my suggestion seriously. "Oh, but, Holt, good catch with the rock from the firepit. The lab was able to confirm it was the murder weapon."

The compliment was unexpected. "Uh, thanks" was all I said.

Paul asked, "Anything else you can tell us?"

"We took a look at the bachelor parties' backpacks and tent." Ranger Trees wiped a tired hand across his face. "But the ranger station is sending crime scene techs to do the official processing of the scene. Our mission is to find Nick."

Sienna leaned forward. "And what about Vincent? Did he tell you anything new after he woke up?"

Ranger Trees stretched. "Nope. He was sad about Kyle and worried about Nick." The ranger half stifled a yawn. "Vincent wanted to help search, but Hagen talked him out of it. He was headed back down to the parking lot when we started hiking up."

We fell silent, each of us lost in our own theories about the murder.

When the water did boil, Paul was the one to pour it into the bags of freeze-dried spaghetti before sealing them and starting his stopwatch. Ranger Trees's eyes had glazed over, and he only refocused when Paul announced, "Food's done."

The ranger nudged Cop Kid. "Hagen."

Extra-loud snore.

"Hagen, wake up. Dinner's ready." While the ranger had joked about Hagen needing to hike more, his forehead was creased as he tried to wake his cousin.

It took some doing, but at last Hagen's eyes partially opened. "Food" was all Ranger Trees said before he began eating out of a spaghetti bag. Cop Kid woke up gradually. He was barely alert when the ranger handed over the second bag. "Here."

Hagen took the bag but didn't start eating.

"Come on." And for once Ranger Trees sounded impatient. "Don't make me feed you."

A spark of humor lit Cop Kid's eyes. And he held out the fork. "Would you?"

Ranger Trees muttered something about "Letting Hagen starve to death" before excusing himself for the privacy of nature.

"Sorry." Cop Kid ran his free hand across his face. "I didn't mean to crash."

I shrugged. "Happens to the best of us."

That earned one of Cop Kid's easy smiles. "I guess it does." Hagen had a few bites of the gross spaghetti before explaining to Paul and Sienna, "We were up late last night." He yawned—like that helped prove his point. "Thorne had requested time off while I visited. But the rangers were already spread thin with that other accident. When they called Thorne in, I tagged along."

Sienna leaned toward the fire. "That puts you in our boat! We're all vacation crime fighters."

She raised her hand in a cheer, but before anyone else could join in, Ranger Trees returned and said dryly, "Leave the crime fighting to the professionals."

My eyes momentarily locked with Hagen's.

He smirked.

We both knew I wasn't about to quit crime fighting.

CHAPTER 12

Ranger Trees stood over us with his arms crossed, resembling a grouchy camp counselor. "No investigating, but since you are witnesses, there's one piece of evidence I needed to ask you about." The ranger took a small digital camera out of his pocket—which interestingly meant pocket-sized cameras were still being made. "Do any of you recognize this?"

He showed me the picture first. It was a pair of plaid men's boxers. "Uh...Paul?"

Paul and Sienna crowded in to take a look.

Sienna giggled.

"Those are mine," Paul said. "Why are they evidence?"

"They were on the body," Ranger Trees said.

"Kyle had the boxers in his pocket," Cop Kid added.

Paul's face transformed into something eerily similar to Britt's paramedic mask. "I had nothing to do with that."

Cop Kid may have built the suspense, but his cousin was quick to jump in. "We know. After you left, we talked with the rangers who hiked up with Vincent." Ranger Trees grimaced. "Apparently, there was a bachelor party game where the goal was to steal something from a camper's backpack and go the longest without being discovered."

"And Kyle stole my underwear?" Paul's voice was raised.

"That's what we're led to believe," the ranger said.

"Hold on." I leaned forward. "Could one of them have stolen a knife out of my bag?"

"Sure," Cop Kid said. "From what the rangers remembered, Kyle stole underwear, Nick stole a knife, and Vincent took water-purifying tablets."

Water-purifying tablets?

Had we packed those?

Paul shook his head. "Those aren't ours. We brought water filters."

"It must be theirs," Ranger Trees said, before walking over to the hiker family.

I couldn't hear everything the ranger said, but I watched Hiker Dad's body language. The man looked ready to jump out of his skin. Could it be the container marked WATER-PURIFYING TABLETS held something more sinister inside?

"Did they play any other games?" Hiker Dad asked. He was trying to play it cool, but his eyes kept darting to where his backpack rested.

Maybe it wasn't the tablets. Because Hiker Dad seemed afraid that something else was discovered when the bros were digging through his bag. Could whatever that was be a motive for murder?

Ranger Trees continued speaking with Hiker Dad. If the ranger was suspicious, he didn't let on.

What kind of immature men-children had party games that involved stealing from strangers?

It explained why my knife had gone missing. And it also meant that Nick had a weapon. Maybe he was a killer, or maybe he was a witness. Either way, he currently wasn't making rational decisions, and I didn't love that he could start stabbing people.

Ranger Trees had just returned when I asked Cop Kid, "Aside from being an underwear thief, did you find out anything about the murder victim?" I expected the ranger would interrupt to say it wasn't my business, but he was rubbing at his eyes like there was sand in them. Just how late had they stayed up last night?

"Ignore him." Hagen jutted his chin in the ranger's direction. "He's not as by the book as he pretends."

Suddenly the ranger's hand was away from his eyes and he was frowning.

Cop Kid just waved his hand dismissively. "Relax. I'm not going to say anything they couldn't discover with Google."

Ranger Trees gave a half nod of acknowledgment before stretching out on the ground with his head and shoulders partially supported by the log I sat on. He'd chosen the spot that was between me and Cop Kid. He didn't smirk or acknowledge either of us, only stared up at the night sky.

"We got a lot of information when we talked to Vincent," Cop Kid said, not at all bothered by his cousin's power play. "The brothers have been friends with him all their lives. They used to be neighbors, but Nick and Kyle's Mom bet against the housing market, and suddenly they were rich."

"But they stayed friends?" Sienna asked from her spot beside Paul.

Ranger Trees's eyes flicked over to her before returning to the night sky.

"Seemed like it." Cop Kid paused to stifle a yawn. His eyes were watering so much, I expected tears would start rolling down his face.

"They weren't always friendly," I said. "Before dinner last night, I overheard an argument between the friend and the murdered brother."

"They were fighting? Holt!" Sienna's eyes were big. "Why didn't you tell us?"

"Yeah," Ranger Trees added. "Why didn't you notify law enforcement?"

I rubbed a hand across my face. "Believe me, it wasn't intentional."

Cop Kid laughed. "I believe it."

"Uh..." Although I'd just heard them, I couldn't remember the names. "The older brother, the one getting married—"

"Nick," Ranger Trees muttered from his spot on the ground.

"Hold on. This is good." Hagen grinned and bent closer, about to reveal a secret. "Nick is marrying Vincent's sister."

Weird. When I'd run into Younger Brother and Broke Friend arguing in the woods, I hadn't gotten the impression they were very close.

Unexpectedly, Ranger Trees stood. "I'm turning in." It was hard to hear his quiet voice above the crackle of the fire.

"That's a good idea." Cop Kid stood up slowly.

I watched as the lawmen walked to their tent. It wasn't like I expected them to stay up all night keeping watch over the campsite. But shouldn't we set up some sort of schedule to keep watch just in case the homicidal hiker decided to strike again?

As if reading my mind, Ranger Trees turned back to us. "I doubt anyone will bother us. But holler if you need anything."

Paul said, "Thanks." And Ranger Trees went and told the hiker family the same thing.

Pretty soon Sienna and the hiker family had also turned in. It left Paul and me sitting opposite each other, staring moodily at the fire.

"Are we safe?" I asked.

Paul leaned back, showing off the broad chest of a commercial fisherman. "Honestly, I think we're more likely to have a bear attack than have to fight a murderer."

I glanced into the dark woods as the night became alive with rustling.

"We're not going to be attacked by bears," Paul added.

"I know." I tried to sound more confident than I was. To change the subject, I asked, "Are you ready for tomorrow?"

Tension Paul had been holding in his shoulders released. "Yeah. This has been a long time coming. I'm so ready."

I half smiled my acknowledgment before continuing to stare at the fire. It was dying down, and the flames were slowly disappearing into bright orange embers.

"After I got arrested, I kept trying to break up with Sienna." Paul's voice was distant, like he was reliving a past life. "But she kept visiting me in jail, kept telling me she knew I was innocent." Paul shook his head. "I was adamant she needed to find someone else. Finally, her parents showed up without her. I was sure they were going to tell me to never speak to her again. But Sienna's mom took my hand, and her dad said they knew I was innocent and Sienna was—" Paul's voice cracked, and he looked up like he'd forgotten I was there. Paul gave a shake of the head but resumed talking. "They said Sienna was lucky to have me in her life."

I swallowed. There was an unusual lump in the back of my throat—must be allergies.

"That visit meant..." Paul trailed off.

We both knew the sentence would remain unfinished.

I ran a hand through my tangled hair. Paul's soon-to-be in-laws thought the very best of him while he was wrongfully in jail.

A sensation almost like nausea swept through me. Due to horrible timing, I met Mrs. Asato during the trip Brittany was kidnapped on. That hadn't been a good first impression. The problem was magnified when Britt chose to leave Oregon to live close to me.

Ever since, Mrs. Asato had tried to avoid me. The one time she visited Seattle, I met them at a restaurant. Right after I arrived, she made Britt take her home because of a headache. Maybe she actually had a headache, but the timing was suspicious, and we never rescheduled during her visit.

It didn't matter what I tried. Mrs. Asato couldn't stand me.

I don't know what gave me away, but Paul said, "My mom can be...Well, anyway...I, uh, don't have a problem with you dating my sister."

One of my eyebrows lifted, though I tried to keep it down.

Paul took a deep breath, like he was about to say something painful. "You're good for her."

I remained skeptical. Call me paranoid, but I kept waiting for him to say something bad.

Paul sighed. "Look, ever since her fiancé died—no, ever since our dad died—Brittany's closed down parts of herself. I didn't think she'd ever go back to the way she was, until you came along..."

I rubbed a hand along my scruffy jaw. I couldn't speak, could barely breathe.

Paul cleared his throat. "Brittany has fun again. If Mom can't see that, it's her problem."

I nodded slowly. I should answer, but what could I say? Finally, I replied with a partial joke. "Thanks for your blessing."

Paul's eyes widened. "It wasn't an official blessing."

I grinned. "Sounded like one."

"Fine." Paul's voice was light as he added, "But I also don't enjoy it when you kiss, or hold hands, or behave at all like you're dating."

We stared at each other from across the fire, then burst out laughing.

"Noted," I said, still chuckling. "But while you may not like it, I'm hoping Britt would have a problem if I stopped kissing, or holding hands, or acting like I'm her boyfriend."

Paul was wiping tears from the corners of his eyes when he admitted, "You're probably right."

———◆◇◆———

We waited until the fire died down before going to bed. Sure, I was tired. I'd been hiking for two days, was undercaffeinated, and had barely slept the night before. While I may have been tired, the problem was, I wasn't *sleepy*.

My sleeping bag remained beside the tent's wall. After last night's experience of a dead hand caressing my head, it was hard to relax. Also, I was worried about Britt. Hopefully her brother was right. She'd gotten overloaded and would feel better after resetting. But if something was truly wrong, how long would it take before we could get help?

And, bears. Why did Paul have to mention bears? I've survived a few encounters with murderers, but I've yet to have a face-off with a bear.

I must've slept, but it was a restless doze that I'd wake up from feeling no time had passed. Paul's snoring had begun almost as soon as he'd zipped his sleeping bag shut. But tonight I don't think the noise made a difference.

It was a relief to have the police at our campsite, yet with how tired Cop Kid and Ranger Trees were, it wasn't like they'd be a great defense system. And while I tried to close my eyes and relax, I couldn't shake the thought that I lay defenseless with a murderer nearby.

It was unbelievably late at night—or incredibly early in the morning—when I finally drifted off into something deeper. The metallic clicking of a zipper had me forcing my eyes open. Was the killer trying to sneak into our tent?

My heart was racing as I waited. But no one was at our tent. Had I imagined the sound?

I lay still, listening. All I heard was Paul's snoring. Was the sound of the zipper an auditory dream?

Then Paul coughed and shifted. For a few seconds his snoring stopped. In that moment of stillness, I heard the metallic sound of a zipper. It was outside the tent, likely where our backpacks were. Could it be a raccoon stealing food, or was it the murderer?

I wanted to raise the alert, but I couldn't disturb Brittany. Plus, last night Paul hadn't been thrilled with the middle-of-the-night wake-up call.

In the game of *would you rather risk confronting a murderer in the woods or risk waking up your girlfriend's brother for a false alarm*? Well, I chose the possible murderer in the woods.

As quietly as possible, I slid out of my sleeping bag before maneuvering around everyone to get to the tent flap. I got my shoes, grabbed a flashlight, and snuck outside.

I kept the light off as I turned the corner of our tent to see our backpacks. Sure enough, something was crouched there. In the darkness, I couldn't tell what the creature was. For a horrifying moment I worried it was a bear. Yet the outline was too small for a bear.

In a moment of brilliance—or sleep-deprived stupidity—I turned on my flashlight right at the creature and yelled, "Hey!"

It took a moment for my brain to process what I was seeing. The two eyes staring back at me belonged to Older Brother. But his hours alone in the wilderness had left him barely recognizable. His eyes were more vacant than Britt's had ever been. Plus, the way he was crouched didn't seem human.

I stared at him, and he stared directly at the flashlight before he let out a strange cry and practically tumbled out of view from the flashlight.

I froze—hopefully not for very long. Should I go after him?

No. I'd end up horribly lost.

Also, whether Older Brother killed Younger Brother or just witnessed the crime, he appeared to be in severe shock, and I didn't have any training for how to deal with that.

I ran to Cop Kid's tent but hesitated at the entrance. *How are you supposed to knock on a tarp?*

"Uh, Hagen...Ranger..."

Before I said anything else, there was rustling, and a gravelly voice said, "Hey, wake up."

Seconds later, Ranger Trees and Cop Kid appeared. Both had shoes on, but the ranger was shirtless. Cop Kid's hair was sticking out at strange angles, while the ranger had a red mark along his cheek—they both were carrying guns.

"What is it?" Ranger Trees asked, squinting at the light from my flashlight.

"The other brother was here. He was by our backpacks."

Ranger Trees took my light and strode to the spot. "Here?" he asked.

I nodded.

The ranger shone the light into the wilderness beyond, his eyes seeming to pick up details I couldn't. Moments later Hagen appeared with their heavy-duty flashlights. Ranger Trees handed back my light.

The ranger was frowning. "Hagen, you stay here. Make sure everyone at the camp stays safe. I'll see if I can find Nick."

"That's a big negatory. You're not going out there alone." Cop Kid sounded laid-back, yet there was an undercurrent of steel in his voice.

The ranger's throat made an impatient sound. "We can't leave the camp unguarded."

Cop Kid was opening his mouth to argue when Paul appeared, also rumpled with sleep. "What's happening?"

Ranger Trees looked him over before asking, "Can you handle yourself?"

Paul stared at him a second before saying, "Yeah."

"Come with me," the ranger said.

Paul followed.

As they disappeared into the trees, Ranger Trees called, "Nick Larkin, this is Idaho Park Ranger Jackson Thorne, come out with your hands up."

It was quite a sight. If I were Older Brother, I don't know what I'd do. Imagine having a shirtless ranger hunting for you in the middle of the night.

"He's in shock," I remembered to yell.

Ranger Trees paused, then gave a slight nod and continued walking with Paul right behind him.

Cop Kid watched them leave. I caught something almost resembling worry on his face. Sensing my attention, Cop Kid's face shifted to his casual smile. "Let's get a fire going. It'll help them find their way back."

"And we can make coffee," I added.

"Sure," Cop Kid agreed absently, his attention shifting back to the flickering flashlight disappearing into the night.

On our way to the firepit, Sienna called, "Holt," quietly, with her head sticking out of the tent.

I bent toward her. "Yeah?"

"Where's Paul?"

"Uhh…" I didn't want to be the one to tell her Paul was chasing a possible killer through the woods. "He's with the ranger."

Sienna was onto me. "And where's Ranger Thorne?"

"In the woods," I admitted. "The older brother was at our camp. They're trying to catch him."

Sienna momentarily squeezed her eyes shut. "I see."

"Hagen's starting a fire, and I'm making coffee," I said. "Do you want to join us?"

"Sure." Sienna disappeared, and when she reappeared, she wore a sweatshirt.

"How's Brittany?" I asked. With all the excitement, I'd forgotten she was resting.

"Still asleep."

"Good," I said.

We joined Hagen right as he got the first sparks of flame. He nodded a greeting to Sienna, then said, "Keep the fire going. I'm going to pack up our tent. Whether or not they find Nick, Thorne and I will be gone once it's daylight."

Cop Kid was about to leave when he asked, "Say, what was Nick doing when you found him?"

My head snapped up. How had I forgotten?

"He was going through our packs."

Sienna stayed to tend the fire while Cop Kid and I walked to the backpacks. The main pocket of my pack yawned open.

"What's missing?" Cop Kid asked as I poked through the contents.

"Uh…" I rubbed a hand across my face. I really needed sleep or coffee.

The main pocket was where I'd stored my food, but that should all be in the bear bag hanging from the tree. I looked up and didn't see the bear bag. A coldness swept through me. With all the excitement, we'd left our food in the backpacks. Might as well have left a sign saying: WELCOME BEARS. FREE FOOD.

"Bears," I muttered.

"What's that?" Cop Kid asked. "*Bears* in your backpack? Like, *gummy bears*?"

I shook my head. "We forgot to hang the food in a bear bag last night. It's lucky we weren't all eaten."

"Holt." Cop Kid momentarily placed a hand on my shoulder. "It's all right. There aren't that many bears out here. Now, do you know what's missing?"

Cop Kid was right. I had to focus. "Let's see." I frowned into my bag. What was inside? "There was trail mix and a freeze-dried meal of meat loaf."

Cop Kid's nose wrinkled. "Meat loaf?"

"Yeah. The meat loaf."

"He was doing you a favor," Cop Kid said. "Trust me, the freeze-dried meat loaf is nasty."

I glared at him.

"Whatever." Hagen chuckled. "Did he steal the coffee powder?"

"Paul has it," I said. Though I hadn't considered the possibility that it could be stolen. If there were no longer any coffee, I'd need to be medevaced out of the wilderness. I sighed when I found Paul's coffee stash. "We're good."

"Great." But Hagen's attention was on the trees, trying to spot movement.

"I didn't know you ever looked serious," I said.

Cop Kid's features immediately relaxed. He shrugged. "I'm only serious once or twice a year."

Chapter 13

T he sky was beginning to lighten by the time Hagen got his tent put away and I had coffee made. I handed Cop Kid a mug of coffee, but he was too busy pacing to drink.

Sienna and I watched Hagen walk back and forth. He'd flattened out his hair, and his gun was unobtrusively holstered.

"Ranger Thorne seemed competent," Sienna whispered, leaning slightly against me.

Somehow Cop Kid heard her. "Oh, Thorne's very competent...But he also has a talent for getting into sticky situations."

"Great." I'd never heard Sienna sound so sarcastic.

"Uh, I'm sure Paul's fine though." Cop Kid tried to smile, but it was way too forced. "They should be back any minute."

They weren't.

The sky was the dusky shade of morning, I was partway through my third cup of coffee, and Cop Kid had sweat trickling down his temples, when the cracking of twigs alerted us to someone's approach.

Sienna and I both stood, and Hagen moved in front of us—his hand resting on his holster.

A moment later Paul and Ranger Trees appeared between the trees. Relief, anger, and exhaustion flashed across Cop Kid's face. Finally, he shook his head and slumped onto the stump.

Sienna gave Paul a hero's welcome, complete with jumping into his arms and kissing him for such an extended period of time, it was a miracle neither one suffocated. Meanwhile, all the ranger got was an annoyed cousin and me.

"We couldn't find him." The ranger's voice held some early-morning gravel. He picked up Cop Kid's now-cooled mug of coffee and took a drink. "If his brain is in full survival mode, he'll wind up at the waterfall."

Hagen grunted.

Ranger Trees was almost apologetic as he asked, "When do you want to leave?"

Cop Kid checked the sky before answering, "With the fire going, let's make oatmeal. It should be plenty bright after that."

Ranger Trees hadn't sat down yet and was still missing a shirt. Hagen stood, offered the ranger the prime real estate of the stump, and walked over to their backpacks.

The ranger sat down with a sigh. Only then did he realize he was missing a shirt.

"Uh, Hagen—" he started to say.

But Cop Kid interrupted. "Already grabbing you a shirt. No one wants to see your muscles."

Half of Ranger Trees's mouth twitched. He said, "At least I have muscles."

Cop Kid ignored the comment. While I have no idea whether Hagen had a six-pack, I do know his clothes hung off him like he was a teenager. When Cop Kid did speak, his words were directed to me. "Thorne saying stuff like that is why you remind me of my cousin."

I tried to look upset, placing my hand dramatically on my heart. "No way I'd ever say something that offensive."

Hagen raised an eyebrow. "My mistake."

Cop Kid rezipped the backpack. The sound triggered a tickling sensation in my temples. Was I missing something?

It wasn't until I'd taken another gulp of coffee that I remembered. This was the second time something was stolen out of my pack. But I wasn't the one with suspicious secrets hidden in the front pocket of my backpack. That was Hiker Dad.

I stood and, in my excitement, collided into Cop Kid as he returned—almost spilling my coffee.

Hagen rubbed at his shoulder as he shook his head. "Holt, you've had enough."

I shook my head. "This has nothing to do with coffee." I quickly explained the strange interaction we'd seen between Uptight Daughter and Hiker Dad.

During story time, Paul and Sienna had rejoined us at the fire. Paul nodded. "Something fishy is going on."

All eyes were on the hiker family's campsite right as Hiker Dad exited his tent.

"Morning," he said, seemingly unbothered by all the attention. Odd, given how sensitive he'd been yesterday morning. Maybe he was behaving since law enforcement was around.

"Morning," Ranger Trees replied. He sounded friendly enough, but from the set of his jaw, he was ready to do battle. He strode confidently to Hiker Dad, with the rest of us following behind. The ranger held his hands slightly up, palms out like that would let Hiker Dad know he wasn't being threatened. "Holt had items stolen from his backpack last night."

Hiker Dad opened his mouth, ready to argue that he wasn't stealing supplies, but the ranger kept talking.

"Is anything missing from your backpacks?"

For a moment Hiker Dad's entire face went slack, like he was about to topple to the ground. Then he gave himself a little shake and moved to where their packs rested against a boulder. Immediately, he had the front zipper open and was removing a decorative container, maybe the size of a kid's jewelry box.

"Oh," Sienna said as soon as the box came into view.

I looked at her questioningly. Did she know what was inside?

"They're ashes," Sienna said quietly.

Hiker Dad met Sienna's gaze. He nodded. "It's my wife."

Suddenly none of us had anything to say. We all did some version of shifting backward, clearing our throats, and staring at the ground.

"It's all right," Hiker Dad said.

Sienna was the first to recover. She made a comment about "Death being a part of life" before wrapping her arms around Hiker Dad.

For a moment he didn't know what to do. Then whatever Sienna's healing energy is hit him, and he gave a half cry before leaning into Sienna, still clutching the ashes.

Paul watched without a hint of jealousy. How could Paul be so okay with his girlfriend kissing men's cheeks and embracing strangers?

Five minutes may have passed before Sienna stepped back. "You'll be okay." The words were a blessing—not a phrase people like me say when at a loss for words.

Hiker Dad quickly wiped under his eyes. "I've been trying to keep it together for the kids, but it's been tough."

"I'll bet." Sienna sounded so sincere, so supportive, my eyes began to water.

"She loved waterfalls," Hiker Dad explained, squeezing the box close to his chest. "We always said we'd take the kids to Infinity Falls, but you know how life is. There was always an excuse for why we were too busy." He gave a shaky breath. "It's too late for her, but we're finally taking the trip as a family."

I asked, "That's why you brought the ashes?" Based on everyone's shocked stares, that was a horribly inappropriate question.

Before anything else was said, the hiker family's tent flapped opened, and Uptight Daughter appeared. She didn't seem concerned to see all of us circled around her dad. But when she saw the box her father was holding, the color drained from her face.

"You told them?" she asked.

Ranger Trees jumped in before Hiker Dad could answer. "Why did you keep it a secret?"

I raised an eyebrow. It was pretty impressive how he'd asked such an open-ended question. Uptight Daughter could find any meaning she wanted.

She fell for it. "I try to avoid telling the police when I plan to commit a crime."

Hiker Dad made a sound that was neither a laugh nor a cry. "All I said was we brought Mom's ashes on this trip to fulfill a promise."

Uptight Daughter glared at the ranger.

But Ranger Trees was unaffected. If anything, his dark eyes were amused. "What crime are you planning on committing?"

At first neither one of them answered. Hiker Dad bowed his head, while his daughter stared stubbornly at nothing. Then Hiker Dad carefully handed the ranger the box of ashes. While Ranger Trees was polite enough to accept the container of human remains, he held the box away from him like any second it might explode.

"We were going to spread her ashes," Hiker Dad admitted.

I spoke for the group when I said, "Umm...?"

Hiker Dad rubbed at his forehead. "My wife loved the symbolism of Infinity Falls."

For some reason, Hiker Dad was looking right at me. I nodded, since sharing my thoughts about a sideways infinity symbol being the number *eight* wasn't appropriate.

"What do ashes in a waterfall have to do with committing a crime?" Ranger Trees asked, delicately holding the container of remains.

"That's the crime." Uptight Daughter huffed. "You're the police. Shouldn't you know that?"

"Er...What?" asked Ranger Trees.

Hiker Dad sighed. "We had the trip all planned when Amanda looked up state park regulations. We're supposed to have a permit. But there wasn't time."

There's a permit for pouring ashes down a waterfall?

"I don't want to go to jail over this," Uptight Daughter said.

Cop Kid suffered a sudden bout of coughing—that sounded eerily similar to laughter.

"Uh..." Ranger Trees's face remained serious, but since he was holding a dead body, it was probably easier to keep a straight face. "Permits for, uh...certain ceremonies isn't something I keep track of." His neck began turning red. "Just don't do anything illegal in front of me."

Hiker Dad let out a breath. "You got it." He took back the ashes. "Thanks for letting me honor my wife's wishes."

The ranger nodded and walked away quickly.

One possible murder theory was out. They weren't transporting a hidden stash of bald eagle feathers. There would be no information for Younger Brother to threaten them with. Neglecting to get a proper permit isn't a strong motive for murder.

———◦———

The police had begun eating oatmeal when Brittany appeared. I was instantly by her side. I wanted to check every part of her to make sure she was okay. From the blank face Britt greeted me with, either she was unwell or worried I'd smother her. I needed to play it cool.

"Morning." I gave her a quick kiss.

Britt tucked a strand of hair behind her ear. "Hey."

Before I could ask any questions, Paul had joined us. "You up to hiking to the falls?"

Brittany raised her eyebrows in such a way as to imply Paul's question was idiotic. I said, "Yes. We're up for hiking."

Paul didn't even waste time replying before he dove into the tent and began packing up our gear.

"He's in a hurry," Britt commented.

What with Paul's desire to leave quickly and Britt determined to show she was in perfect health, we left the campsite shortly after the police.

I never really thought of myself as scared of the dark, but on this trip I'd had a horrible time sleeping at night—granted, murderers lurking behind trees doesn't help. But whatever the disconnect, this morning my brain determined it was safe to doze off since the sun was up. It took all my concentration to keep my eyes open and stay on the trail.

I tried to walk at the pace Paul and Sienna were going, but I kept lagging behind. Britt was the one having to match my speed.

Once, when I wandered *slightly* off trail, she grabbed my elbow and said, "You're the one we should worry about." Her twin was right. A good night's sleep and Britt was back to being herself.

I didn't answer. Only blinked at her, trying to focus.

"Did you get any sleep last night?"

I shrugged. "A little."

"Uh-huh." Britt was frowning, outlining the scar by her eyebrow. "Did you find out anything interesting about the case?"

"Mm...yeah? I think so."

Britt tugged my arm, and we resumed walking. "What did you learn?"

My brain was fuzzy, but I did my best to recap. Britt's lips pressed together when I told her about Paul disappearing into the woods hunting for Older Brother. When I detailed how uncomfortable the ranger was holding a container of ashes, a laugh escaped Britt.

She covered her mouth and shook her head. "I'm sorry. It really isn't funny, but..." She trailed off, her eyes sparkling with amusement.

Britt tried to keep me talking. It helped, yet my attention kept drifting, and I wasn't the best companion.

Once I thought I heard the clinking of a pebble rolling behind us. I ignored it. But a few minutes later there was the crack of a twig snapping. I spun around.

"What's wrong?" Britt asked.

"Are we being followed?"

"No?" Britt stood beside me and looked down at what we could see of the trail. "At least, I don't think so."

"I keep hearing things." And while I couldn't see any figures creeping closer, there was a tingling along my spine that made me shudder. I was missing something.

Britt suggested, "The Caffreys are also going to the falls. Maybe you heard them."

"Maybe."

We resumed hiking. A new round of paranoia was the jolt I needed to wake up. I was more alert and kept peering behind me, expecting to catch movement. But there was nothing.

The sun was getting high in the sky when I first noticed the distant crash of water. We had to be close to Infinity Falls. As we walked, the sound gradually grew louder, yet the waterfall refused to come into view.

The sound was dreadful. It promised rest while remaining an unknown distance away. I was in such a grumpy mood that by the time Infinity Falls came into view, I was too annoyed to care.

It was bigger than I'd expected. It was nothing compared to Niagara Falls, but it was a respectable waterfall. Probably worth the trip if you enjoyed spending time in nature. It was also easy to spot the number eight—or the *sideways* infinity symbol—thanks to two massive outcroppings of rocks.

"We'll set up camp near the top of the waterfall," Britt said.

I nodded. At that point, I wasn't surprised I'd need to hike up a steep grade to get to the campsite.

Up ahead, Paul was practically jogging up the tight switchback in his hurry to set up camp. After all, he had a proposal to get to.

Paul was always efficient in setting up camp. But today it was like he was on a game show, competing for a million dollars. He practically finished building the tent before I'd zipped shut my backpack after handing over the tent poles.

Once he'd tossed the sleeping bags haphazardly inside, he smiled to himself and turned around to find us all staring at him.

"What's the rush?" Britt asked.

Paul was too worked up to notice her eyes were twinkling. "No rush," he lied. "Who's hungry?"

We all shared amused glances as Paul got us granola bars. Couldn't he tell everyone knew he was going to propose?

He tried to sit down and eat with the rest of us, but he was too agitated to chew. He kind of coughed down a bite before jumping to his feet and pacing.

Paul was *very* bad at playing it cool. And Sienna was a guaranteed yes. Were proposals always so stressful?

Sienna was halfway through her granola bar when Paul blurted, "Sienna, would you like to see the waterfall?"

For a moment Sienna stilled. She touched her head, making sure all her dreadlocks were in place. "Um, yes. Of course."

Was Sienna nervous, too?

She stood up and gently lowered Paul's head toward her. She brushed her fingers along his temple. "You're sweating."

"Yeah, well, I have something important to ask you." Paul took Sienna's hand and kissed it. Then he must have been so taken with the moment, he couldn't wait for privacy or the view of the waterfall we'd nearly broken our necks to see. In a second he'd dropped to one knee, fumbling with the zipped pocket of his shorts.

I hadn't been expecting the show and half choked as I swallowed wrong. Britt wordlessly handed me water, but her focus remained on the couple.

Paul's voice was deep as he said, "Sienna, I had a million things I wanted to say to you. But it all boils down to this. I love you. I want to spend the rest of my life with you." He held up a ring. "Will you marry me?"

Sienna opened her mouth, but no sound came out. Instead, she nodded yes over and over again. A moment later Paul was on his feet, swinging her up into his arms. They were both crying.

I stood and offered Britt a hand up. This moment was too personal to be shared with anyone else.

Britt and I followed a trail that led along the cliff.

Once we were far enough away from the happy couple, I exhaled. "Glad that proposal's over with."

Had I said that out loud?

Would Britt think I was opposed to marriage?

"That's not...I didn't mean—" Before I could dig myself any deeper, the police came into view.

"Have you found Nick?" Britt asked.

Ranger Trees shook his head. "No, but we think he's close."

A sound resembling a yell echoed against the crashing of the waterfall. It was impossible to track the origin.

That wasn't good.

Each of us looked around, trying to guess where the sound came from.

"Where should we look?" Cop Kid asked his cousin.

The ranger's eyes were half-closed as he thought. "I can't say for sure. But that was shouting from a fall. We'll want to keep a close eye around the cliffs."

It wasn't like Ranger Trees actually said, *We should split up.* Yet the two of them went off in opposite directions. I turned to ask Britt where she wanted to search, but Britt was gone.

Fear tightened my chest. Was she in danger? I checked the area around me for clues. In the dust was a clear imprint of Britt's small boot facing the direction of our camp. She must be checking that Paul and Sienna were safe. I considered following her, yet if Ranger Trees was correct and a person lay injured, the faster they were found, the better.

I walked along the rocky edge with the sun behind me. The drop past the waterfall was less severe, yet it would make a nasty landing.

In the sunlight, the fear from last night was gone. Even if Older Brother was the killer, by now he'd been reduced to a man who'd snuck into a camp to steal freeze-dried meat loaf.

Maybe Older Brother really was the killer. If he was a witness, why had he run?

As I continued peering over the cliffside, the first thing I spotted was a strange, almost sandy rock with waves of...hair. A hand was the next thing flopped near the head. The rest of the body took shape. Older Brother lay among the rocks beneath me.

He'd been lucky enough to fall on an outcropping, which meant the drop was closer to twenty or thirty feet.

Older Brother's left leg was twisted at an unnatural angle, and he wasn't moving. In one hand he gripped the stolen knife, but the blade wasn't open.

"Hey," I called. "Can you hear me?"

There was no reaction. Older Brother remained motionless.

"Wake up!"

His fingers twitched, and he gave a faint cough.

Alive. I'd found him alive.

"Hang on," I shouted. "Help is on the way."

I'd spoken too soon.

When I turned to leave, I found Broke Friend standing in front of me. I gulped in a breath.

This might be bad.

CHAPTER 14

"You're here" was all I could think to say.

How had the man who'd passed out by our fire yesterday had the stamina to make it all the way to Infinity Falls? Unfortunately, he was holding a very large hunting knife…Actually, when does a knife become a dagger or a small sword? Whatever the size, the knife Broke Friend had pointed at me should be considered a dagger.

Broke Friend seemed in no mood for small talk. He took a step forward while I took a step back, before remembering I was dangerously near a ledge with a steep drop.

"Easy" is what Broke Friend said. He held one hand up like he was harmless and tucked the hand with the dagger behind his back. Even without the knife, I suspected that if I said the wrong thing, he'd shove me over the edge and I'd be in the same predicament as Older Brother.

"You must be lost," I said, trying to mirror Broke Friend's forced casualness. "The parking lot is in the opposite direction."

"Thanks," Broke Friend said in a similarly neutral tone. Not that it mattered. Neither one of us bought the other's performance. "I was headed back down when I realized I couldn't live with myself if I went home while Nick was dying in the wilderness."

"Such a good friend." I sounded sarcastic, but Broke Friend didn't notice.

Based on Broke Friend's behavior, it seemed likely he was the killer. Older Brother must've watched the murder and fled the campsite. This whole time Broke Friend had been trying to find Older Brother, to silence him before he could tell the police what happened.

I eyed Broke Friend. This was going to be tricky.

If he'd pushed Older Brother over the ledge, he probably thought Older Brother was dead instead of severely injured. As far as Broke Friend knew, he'd just gotten away with a double murder. Could I keep up the charade until the police arrived?

The moment my idea formed, a groan echoed up from where Older Brother lay. I tried to hide the sound by coughing, but it was too late. The damage was done.

"Nick's alive." Any pretense of being worried evaporated from Broke Friend's face. "You're not surviving this." His voice was calm and matter-of-fact. He sounded like an accountant commenting on the increased value of stocks.

I crept slightly away from the ledge. As I moved, Broke Friend squinted.

Interesting.

He had to face the sun to look at me. I didn't know how, but I'd have to use that.

For starters, I decided to play a little dumb. I ignored his comment about my impending doom and pointed over the cliff.

"I don't know what you're talking about. But your friend needs help."

"I know he's there." Broke Friend pointed the knife at me and took a terrifying step closer. "I'm the one who pushed him."

I swallowed. If I survived this, I could give a statement saying Broke Friend confessed to shoving his friend. Now all I needed was for him to admit to killing Younger Brother.

Time to attempt empathy. What had Cop Kid said about money? "Uhh, it's awful your friends got all the money because of their mom. People with money can be so...annoying."

Broke Friend stared in my general direction, but I don't know what he saw with the sun in his eyes.

Assuming my empathy plan had failed, I was trying to come up with a new way to connect with him, when Broke Friend nodded. "They turned into brats when they got rich."

When he said *brat*, I couldn't help the snort of laughter. Immediately, Broke Friend's posture went rigid. "Sorry." I held up my hands. "I get it. My baby sister can be a major brat."

"Not as bad as those two," Broke Friend stated.

"Uh-huh." Miraculously, I kept the sarcasm from my voice. Difficult to do given Broke Friend's total commitment to *woe is my life*.

"They wouldn't even loan me money." Broke Friend's voice was bitter. "Kyle kept saying I needed to pay back what I already owed him. But I kept telling him I needed more money to finish the diving project. Once we found the treasure, we'd be rich."

Diving? Found the treasure? Kyle, at one point, had actually loaned money for an underwater treasure hunt?

Also, what were the chances that Cop Kid or Ranger Trees would find me before Broke Friend grew bored of talking and went for the kill?

"Were you arguing the night he died?" I asked.

"Yeah." For half a second Broke Friend almost looked sad. "Kyle and I just kept fighting. It was bumming Nick out, so I left."

He left...? Like, *before* the murder. He had to be lying—unless Broke Friend had told the truth but not the *whole truth*.

"But you came back?"

The knife Broke Friend held faltered. "Kyle had to see he was making a mistake. All I did was wait for Nick to fall asleep. Then I got Kyle to leave the tent so we could talk in private."

"No." For the first time I contradicted him, and I even took a step closer. "You created an alibi for yourself by leaving camp. You didn't come back to *have another conversation with Kyle.*"

Broke Friend inhaled shakily, but when he exhaled, it was like he'd figured something out. "Fine. I *meant* to kill him. I *wanted* to kill him. I *enjoyed* killing him."

And there was my confession for premeditated murder. If I weren't still in danger, I would have given myself a modest round of applause.

"It's my bad luck that Nick woke up and saw me do it. He would've given me the loan once Kyle was out of the way. But then Nick freaked out. I tried to grab him in the tent. We wrestled, and he ran away. I had to waste my time looking for him before he told anyone."

The memory of dead fingers brushing across my head made me ask, "Why did you move the body?"

"Time." He sounded whiny. "All I needed was time. None of you were supposed to find Kyle. It could've been days before he was discovered. There didn't need to be police hounding my every move. But somehow you stumbled on him when you went to go pee."

I wanted to clarify that I discovered the body thanks to my superb detective skills—not a weak bladder—but I stayed silent.

"If I could hide Kyle's body and silence Nick before he started blabbing, no one could pin this on me."

I couldn't help saying, "No one could arrest you for the murders *you* committed?"

"Exactly." Somehow Broke Friend thought I was agreeing with him. "I thought Nick would go down the mountain to call the police. Why would he go farther up?"

My guess was that watching his best friend kill his brother had thrown off Older Brother's rational thinking. I kept that to myself since the question seemed rhetorical.

Another moan came from below us.

Broke Friend's eyes hardened. It was time. He was about to kill me.

My options were limited to fall, flee, freeze, fight with my body—or fight with my brain. I decided to use my brain.

If it came to it, I'd do everything in my power to take the knife away. For now I'd start with the option with the lowest chance of getting stabbed.

Broke Friend was about to lunge at me. "Wait!" My voice was low and surprisingly commanding. He hesitated, and I blurted a semi-believable excuse. "There's a skunk."

"So?" Broke Friend tried to sound unbothered, but he couldn't hide the curl of his lip at the word *skunk*.

"If you come at me, I will fight back. The skunk is...there." I gestured to a nearby spot somewhat hidden from Broke Friend's view by a boulder. Hopefully the rock, the sun in his eyes, and my superb acting skills would convince him. "If we start fighting, what do you think the chances are the skunk will spray?"

"I don't care if I get sprayed," Broke Friend said, but he was shifting backward.

"If you're sprayed, law enforcement will be able to smell you from a mile away. It wouldn't matter how fast you ran. They'd find you."

Broke Friend's stare was cold, then desperate. Finally, he muttered something to himself and ran off.

I was about to sprint in the opposite direction, when I got an adrenaline crash. My knees buckled, and I spent a few seconds dry heaving before I could get help. I hadn't gone far when Ranger Trees called my name. It took me a moment to spot him, since he'd been partly camouflaged by nature.

"I found them," I panted—extra winded from the higher elevation. "The friend is the murderer. He pushed the older brother off a ledge." My words came in such a rush, I barely understood myself.

Ranger Trees stared at me for a few seconds. "Is Nick alive?"

"Last I checked."

He nodded and turned on his radio. "This is park ranger Jackson Thorne. I'm requesting an immediate medevac at Infinity Falls."

In the minute it took Ranger Trees to give the operator all the important information, Cop Kid showed up with Britt, Paul, and Sienna. "What happened?" Cop Kid asked, sounding laid-back though his body was poised for action.

"Vincent is a fugitive on the run, and a medevac helicopter is en route for Nick." Ranger Trees spoke quickly as I led the way to the drop where Older Brother lay.

Britt said, "I need to get down there."

Ranger Trees gave a slight shake of his head. Before he could open his mouth, Britt added, "I'm a licensed paramedic."

A spark of amusement flashed through Ranger Trees, and for a moment his darker features almost resembled his cousin's. "Well, I'm certified in first aid." He began digging through his pack and brought out a large coil of rope. "Let me know if you want help."

"Or if there's room on the ledge," I added. I wasn't exactly a fan of Britt hanging suspended by a rope over a long drop, but the ranger overcrowding the already narrow ledge was unnecessary.

While Paul and Ranger Trees were securing Britt into a makeshift harness, Cop Kid pulled me aside. "Which way did he go?"

I was so focused on Britt, it took me a moment to understand the question was about Broke Friend. But once I'd figured it out, I pointed down the trail.

"Thanks." Hagen winked. "See you soon."

"He has a knife," I warned.

"And I have a gun."

Ranger Trees was so focused on getting Britt ready for her descent that his eyes widened with Cop Kid's parting call. "Hagen?" His voice was eerily quiet.

"Chasing the murderer," I said.

"I see." Ranger Trees couldn't look away from his cousin's disappearing figure, yet he took a step closer to the rope attached to Brittany, like he knew his duty was with us.

"Go," Paul said. "We got this."

For a moment the ranger's eyes seemed to darken as he considered his options. Finally, he said, "Thanks," before jogging off to catch up with Cop Kid.

Paul had the rope secured around a tree. "You ready?"

"Almost," Britt said. Before I had time to react, Britt's hands were in my hair and we were kissing. "I love you," she whispered.

"I love you, too," I replied automatically. By the time my brain had caught up to realize that little display of affection was because she was about to go rock climbing in a homemade harness, she was already at the side of the cliff with Paul feeding her just enough rope so that she could be horizontal with the rock wall.

I tried to move and be a second set of hands holding the rope that was Britt's lifeline, yet I had to wait for the sudden nausea to lessen before I could lend a hand...The upset stomach must be from all the freeze-dried food. It couldn't be from watching my girlfriend disappear over the side of a cliff.

CHAPTER 15

When I was finally able to move, I peered over the edge. Britt was almost to Older Brother. Paul lowered the rope a few more feet, and Britt made it safely onto the ledge beside him.

Britt asked him a question.

He groaned.

At least he was alive.

I tried to watch. To be ready in case Britt needed help. But staring down made me dizzy. It was Sienna who took my hand and led me to a patch of shade. "Have some water."

After a few sips that did nothing to settle my stomach, I nodded toward the ring on her left hand. "Congratulations."

I expected Sienna to say *Thank you*, but what actually happened was Sienna shoving her hand in my face. "Isn't the ring amazing? Paul designed it specially for me."

"I've never seen anything like it," I said. Which was true. The ring was mostly light blue stones with tiny diamonds.

"They're our birthstones," Sienna said. "Aquamarine and diamonds. White and blue like the ocean where we met."

"Impressive."

What I couldn't tell was whether Sienna was giving me all the details about her ring because she was trying to distract me from Britt being in danger or if she was so excited about getting engaged, she couldn't help sharing with her fiancé's sister's boyfriend.

"Oh, look," Sienna said.

Instead of her ring, she was pointing to the trail. Through the trees came law enforcement with Broke Friend walking between them in handcuffs.

"Will you take Vincent to camp?" Ranger Trees asked his cousin.

Hagen nodded and continued walking with the prisoner while the ranger joined Paul at the cliff's edge.

"The chopper should be here in around five minutes," he called down. "How's he doing?" I couldn't hear Britt's reply, but Ranger Trees nodded like it was good news.

"After Nick gets medevaced, they'll send another helicopter to pick up me, Hagen, and Vincent," Ranger Trees told us.

"Thanks for helping out when you were supposed to be on vacation," Paul said.

The ranger nodded, but his ears were red and his focus was on the ground. Seemed he wasn't a fan of being appreciated. What would happen if Sienna tried to kiss his cheek?

The distant thunder of the chopper broke through the crashing from the waterfall. Once it reached us, it hovered above, causing wind that made the trees twist in strange directions. Something resembling a giant basket was lowered down to the ledge where Britt waited with the injured man.

I returned to the edge of the cliff. As sickening as the whole ordeal was, it was kind of sexy watching Britt do her job in such a treacherous environment.

My head filled with pressure from the chopper above me, but I stayed as close to Britt as I could. It wasn't like she needed my help, or even that I'd be able to help, yet I was close by.

And it was impressive. The way Britt worked in her limited space, you'd think she did mountain rescues all the time. Once she'd gotten Older Brother inside the basket and secured straps across him, she signaled the chopper and they began the careful process of raising the basket.

When the basket was lifted to around Britt's shoulder, a gust of wind caused it to swing wildly. Britt ducked before it knocked her over. After that the basket was quickly raised the rest of the way before disappearing into the helicopter.

My eyes began to sting. At first I thought it was tears. Then I realized I was sweating so much, it was rolling into my eyes. I've heard of *panic attacks*, but is there such a thing as a *sweating attack*?

I needed to stay calm until Britt was back on solid ground.

We waited until after the helicopter had flown away before discussing the best way to bring Britt back up. In the absence of the thundering helicopter, I could hear myself think again—though all of us were talking louder due to some temporary hearing loss.

Brittany wanted to climb the wall, but thankfully Ranger Trees and Paul talked her out of it. In the end—after a lot of back-and-forth—it was agreed we'd lift her up while Britt braced off the rock wall as she made the ascent.

It didn't take us long to lift her out, and once she was safely standing in front of me, I nearly suffocated her in a bear hug.

"Don't do stupid stuff," I murmured.

I felt Britt's laugh instead of hearing it.

She said, "I love you, too." Once I finally let go, Britt handed the ranger a string pack and Paul's knife. "I'm not sure if the knife is evidence. And this bag was in the basket when they lowered it. It says your name."

His mouth twitched, but the rest of his face remained serious. "This must be Hagen's grocery list."

Why had I expected he'd give an explanation?

On the walk back to camp, Sienna started talking about her wedding. Britt was more than willing to discuss details. At our campsite, Britt, Sienna, and Paul all sat together, yet I made a point of *not* joining. No way was I getting dragged into hour-long debates about band versus DJ. Already Paul's eyes were glazed over, and they'd only discussed the bridal party.

Sienna said something about *maid of honor*, and Britt practically squealed, "I'd love to."

"We'll want an even number of bridesmaids and groomsmen," Sienna said. "Paul, how many groomsmen can you have?"

It took a moment for Paul to process that the question was actually directed at him. "Uh, well, there's Isaac, and—"

"Are you having an outdoor wedding?" Britt interrupted, and Paul lapsed into silence.

Their conversation was entertaining to watch as an observer. Though I might die if I had to participate. My focus was so locked in, I didn't notice when Hagen walked up.

Cop Kid stood at my shoulder, observing the wedding planning. Based on how his eyes crinkled, he was also amused.

We stood together, enjoying the private show that none of the players were aware they were putting on. The waterfall was roaring in the background, and the ranger was keeping a close watch on the unrepentant Broke Friend.

It was my closest moment to finding peace in nature. And with peace came sleepiness. I yawned as my body remembered how little sleep I'd gotten on this trip.

My yawn caught Cop Kid's attention. "I almost forgot. I had a couple of gifts delivered."

"Prime shipping goes anywhere?"

Cop Kid laughed. "Something like that." He held the string pack from the helicopter. "First"—he took out an item hidden in his fist—"I wanted you to have a bear sighting after spending so much time in the woods." Cop Kid opened his hand to reveal a silver grizzly bear key chain.

"Very funny." I tried to sound unimpressed, but I couldn't hide my grin as Hagen handed me the key chain.

"Next"—he rifled through the pack and pulled out a food packet of freeze-dried meat loaf—"I wouldn't want you to miss out on fine dining. And, finally"—a can of Starbucks double shot blinded me—"I thought you could use some real coffee."

My hand actually trembled as I took it from Hagen. "Are you sure?"

He didn't bother answering, only watched with the amused expression that was perpetually on his face. The can was open and half-gone in a matter of seconds. I could have chugged it all at once, but I forced myself to savor the rest.

Who am I kidding? I meant to savor the second half, but in reality the whole thing was gone in under a minute.

I sighed, already feeling the espresso at work. "Thank you. You're, like, my favorite person."

Cop Kid raised his eyebrows. "Can I tell Brittany that?"

"If you explain the espresso, she'll understand."

The tension headache I'd tried to ignore began easing away. "You know, you could have sold me that at a ridiculous markup. Like, my starting bid would have been a hundred dollars, but I would have gone higher."

"I'll keep that in mind for next time."

"Hagen?" Ranger Trees approached with the handcuffed Broke Friend. "The helicopter wants to pick us up about a mile and a half west of here. We should get going."

"Sure thing." Cop Kid waited until the pair had left to say, "It's too bad I'll miss the wedding talk. Any minute they're bound to start discussing the pros and cons of baby's breath."

My eyes were watering as I tried not to yawn. "Shame you have to go."

"Wanna tell them your opinions on baby's breath?"

I stared at him. Was he kidding? With Hagen, it was sometimes hard to tell. "As tempting as that sounds, I'm going to bed."

For once, Cop Kid actually looked surprised. "After a double shot of espresso?"

"Absolutely. Now I'm relaxed enough to sleep."

Hagen stared at me for a moment while he tried to figure out if I was serious. He shook his head and laughed. "All right, then." Cop Kid held out his hand. "Until the next dead body."

We shook.

"Until the next dead body."

CIVILIZATION

I t was late afternoon two days later when we arrived back at the parking lot. I returned basically unchanged...The biggest difference was that my five o'clock shadow had turned into the start of a beard.

I'd confirmed just how much I like technology and indoor plumbing. Also, Cop Kid and Ranger Trees were right. Freeze-dried meat loaf is disgusting.

Juniper and Jude's vehicle was parked. They were in the picnic area while Juniper filmed herself with her dog. While Jude immediately noticed our arrival, it was Chouzie barking that alerted my sister.

Juniper stopped recording and bounded toward us. She was headed straight to me, yet Sienna intercepted her. "I'm getting married!"

My sister started screaming and jumping up and down. She was about to attack hug Sienna when Jude took Chouzie's leash away. The poor chow chow wasn't prepared for that much excitement.

"It looks like Sienna stole your welcome home," Brittany said.

I shrugged. "Sienna's excited about the wedding. Pretty soon she'll be showing Jude the ring and explaining the birthstones."

As I spoke the words, Sienna held her hand out, and Juniper was giving the engagement ring a close inspection.

"Juniper's confirming her ring's bigger," I said quietly enough so only Britt heard.

"Of course she cares about that," Britt said.

"Something wrong with that?" I asked, having a strange urge to defend my sister.

"Well…" Britt's eyes flicked shyly up at me. "I guess there's nothing wrong with your sister appreciating the money Jude spent on her ring. Still, I'd rather have a ring like Sienna's that held meaning instead of a showpiece." Britt flushed and began tucking invisible strands of hair behind her ears.

Wait a second.

Was that…a hint?

Did Britt *want* to marry me?

Had we been together long enough?

Before I could investigate further, Sienna was calling, "Brittany, come here. Juniper had the best idea. We could use baby's breath…" I didn't bother paying attention to the rest.

I'd set my backpack by their SUV when Juniper half-tackle-hugged me from behind.

"Juniper," I grunted as I struggled to keep us both from splatting onto the pavement.

"Ew!" Juniper wrinkled her nose and took a step back. "You smell."

I raised an eyebrow. "I don't have clean clothes and I haven't showered in days. What did you expect?"

Juniper tossed her hair. "I don't know. I didn't think you'd survive the trip, so I never guessed how you'd smell after."

I tried to run a hand through my hair, but it was tangled and matted down. "Well, thanks for believing in me."

Juniper ignored the sarcasm. "What was the scariest part? People at the hotel said there was a murder. Did you help solve it? Were there bears?"

For the moment I wasn't ready to relive the mystery. The dead hand caressing my head still sent tingles down my spine. Instead, I said, "No bears, but Sienna and I had to fight off a skunk."

"Oh." Juniper giggled. "Is that why you smell so bad?"

I rolled my eyes. "Do you want to hear the story?"

Juniper nodded, and by the end she was clutching her stomach with tears streaming down her cheeks. "No!" she gasped. "That's awful."

I grinned. "If you think I smell now, imagine how much worse it could have been."

Juniper wiped the tears from her face. "Imagine if Paul had proposed while Sienna reeked of skunk."

"Yeah. That would've been memorable."

Juniper took a deep breath as her laughter died down. "It's probably for the best that the skunk behaved. This way they have a cute story."

"And," I added, "Paul was able to get close enough to put the ring on her finger."

"She *loves* that ring." Juniper's nose scrunched. While I expected her to say some version of *my ring's better*, she surprised me by saying, "Your birthday's in April."

I stared at her. Seeing as it was June, any birthday celebration would either be super late or very early. "Uh, yeah. Why?"

"Well, Britt and Paul obviously have the same birthday because they're twins. Their birthstone is aquamarine. And since your birthday's in April and Sienna's birthday's in April, you could propose to Britt with an exact duplicate of Sienna's ring."

Propose? Juniper had just said *propose* with my girlfriend nearby?

Also, *matching engagement rings*? When Britt said she wanted a ring to have meaning, I don't think she meant the exact ring her sister in-law had.

I'm pretty sure Juniper was kidding...Still, it sounded awfully cringy.

"Holt?" Juniper asked.

"Matching rings?" I frowned. "I'd need to ask Paul where he got his made. But I'll get right on that."

Juniper's face went slack from shock. "You will?"

"No!" I frowned. "I'm not giving Brittany the ring her brother designed. That would be...weird."

"But, are you"—Juniper dropped her voice real low—"going to propose?"

Was I?

Before Brittany, I'd assumed I'd live and die a bachelor. But now? Waking up every day with Britt at my side, getting to call her my wife, and possibly a couple of baby Brittanys running around...Instead of sounding bad or scary, it made me...excited.

I wanted to marry Brittany Asato.

Why had it taken Paul's proposal and Juniper's teasing to make me realize it?

Who knows what my face was doing, but Juniper grew tired of waiting for my answer. "Come on, Holt. What's holding you back?"

I didn't answer immediately. My gaze wandered to where Britt was talking excitedly with Sienna. A warmth spread through my chest. I couldn't stop my smile.

"Nothing," I said. "Nothing's holding me back."

I was ready to propose.

———◀◯▶———

Will Holt find his missing engagement ring and catch a killer before he leaves Australia? Read _A Not So Perfect Proposal_ to find out!

Ready for a Holt Jacobs snack-sized mystery? Sign up for my newsletter at _lilystirling.com_ and receive a copy of _Holt Jacobs & The Mystery Of The Missing Sunglasses,_ plus delightful every-other-week emails.

Cheers!

Congratulations! You've just crossed off a book on your *To Be Read* list.

I hope you loved *A Not So Happy Camper*! It would really help me (and potential readers) if you rated and reviewed this book.

I've only gone backpacking once. I was twelve years old, and it was a youth trip.

At the time, I had every intention of backpacking again. However, on this trip, the "more experienced teenage hikers" managed to get lost for a few hours.

Everyone was safely reunited. Yet the trip was upsetting enough that the youth leaders never brought another group of teens into the wilderness.

While, yes, as an adult, I can now figure out a way to safely go backpacking, I have enough Holt-like tendencies to be quite happy typing about the great outdoors from the safety of my computer—seriously, tents are not secure.

Next up is *A Not So Perfect Proposal*, where Holt lands himself in the middle of a mystery in Australia. He'd planned an elaborate engagement but finds himself chasing down clues while trying to find his engagement ring and catch a killer.

If you're interested in staying in touch with me and my books, I'd love it if you'd join my every other week newsletter at *lilystirling.com*.

You'll receive delightful updates and a copy of *Holt Jacobs & The Mystery of the Missing Sunglasses*—where he solves what happened to his sunglasses in a crowded airport.

Thanks for reading. It's been a pleasure!

~ *Lily Stirling*

P.S. I have no idea if freeze-dried meatloaf is disgusting...I can say I didn't enjoy freeze-dried spaghetti.

ACKNOWLEDGEMENTS

I'm so grateful for everyone on my production team. Thanks for all you do!

Developmental Editor ~ Kristen Weber

Copyeditor ~ Penina Lopez

Cover Designer ~ Mariah Sinclair

———————●○●———————

A huge thanks goes to my family for all your love and support. You're wonderful listeners, readers...and occasional conspiracy theorists—always ready to make suggestions on future stories.

To my author friends Bellamina Court and Jess Corbeau, I'm so happy to be a *Moonshine Girl* with the two of you. I can't imagine lovelier people to write a book series with. Co-authoring *Murder & Moonshine* and *Poison & Pumpkin Spice* has been a blast!

Thanks to Alessandra, Terezia, Eva, and my author friends at Inkers Mastermind. It's been incredible to have such a supportive writing community.

Finally, thank *you* for reading my book and all the back matter. I hope you love *A Not So Happy Camper* as much as I do!

Until next time!
Lily Stirling

ABOUT THE AUTHOR

L ily Stirling is the writer of the Holt Jacobs Mystery series and co-author of the Moonshine Girls Mysteries.

She spent a quarter of a century living in the Pacific Northwest. Lily was born in Idaho, but her family moved to Washington around the time she could read chapter books.

Mysteries have always delighted her, from listening to The Hardy Boys on car trips to watching episodes of Psych.

As for sarcastic families, when she's not writing about one, she's living in one.

HOLT JACOBS MYSTERY SERIES

A Not So Shocking Murder
A Not So Rustic Retreat
A Not So Rosy Vintage
A Not So Cozy Christmas
A Not So Simple Seminar
A Not So Happy Camper
A Not So Perfect Proposal

———◄O►———

Holt Jacobs isn't for everyone. He's a sarcastic introvert who can never get quite enough coffee. Becoming a sarcastic sleuth was unexpected, but as an engineer, Holt is used to solving puzzles.

MOONSHINE GIRLS MYSTERY SERIES

Murder & Moonshine
Poison & Pumpkin Spice

———◆O◆———

Moonshine Girls Davie Carter, Fenn Everhart, and Daisy Mae Harper met over moonshine and have been friends ever since. They'd planned on distilling, transporting, and selling illegal hooch but keep stumbling over crimes and solving mysteries.

———◆O◆———

The Moonshine Girls Mystery Series are intertwined anthologies written by Lily Stirling, Bellamina Court, and Jess Corbeau.

www.ingramcontent.com/pod-product-compliance
Lightning Source LLC
Chambersburg PA
CBHW032212170626
46808CB00006B/2440